# "I need to apologize, Jacob…"

Hannah glanced up at Jacob, and then away. "I was rude to you yesterday, and I'm very sorry. I know better than to speak harshly, let alone to someone who is being kind to us."

"It's my fault. I stuck my nose where it didn't belong."

Now she laughed outright. "Perhaps you did, but it was probably something I needed to hear."

"Apology accepted."

*"Danki."*

*"Gem gschene."* The age-old words felt curiously intimate, shared there on the bench with the sun slanting through golden trees.

"It's a fine line," Hannah said. "Giving him the extra attention and care his condition requires, but not being overly protective. I'm afraid I'm still learning."

"You're doing a *wunderbar* job."

Which caused her to smile again, and then suddenly the tension that had been between them was gone.

He realized that what Hannah was offering with her apology was a precious thing—her friendship.

For now, he needed to be satisfied with that.

**Vannetta Chapman** has published over one hundred articles in Christian family magazines, receiving over two dozen awards from Romance Writers of America chapter groups. She discovered her love for the Amish while researching her grandfather's birthplace of Albion, Pennsylvania. Her first novel, *A Simple Amish Christmas*, quickly became a bestseller. Chapman lives in the Texas Hill Country with her husband.

### Books by Vannetta Chapman

### Love Inspired

### *Indiana Amish Brides*

*A Widow's Hope*

# A Widow's Hope

## Vannetta Chapman

HARLEQUIN® LOVE INSPIRED®

Recycling programs
for this product may
not exist in your area.

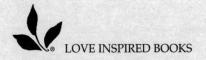

LOVE INSPIRED BOOKS

ISBN-13: 978-1-335-42822-6

A Widow's Hope

www.Harlequin.com

Printed in U.S.A.

And we know that all things work together
for good to them that love God.
—*Romans* 8:28

The Lord hath heard my supplication;
the Lord will receive my prayer.
—*Psalms* 6:9

This book is dedicated to JoAnn King, who has recently become an avid reader. JoAnn, you're a constant source of encouragement and joy. Thank you for your friendship.

## Acknowledgments

I would like to thank Melissa Endlich for inviting me to join the wonderful group of authors at Harlequin/Love Inspired. I'd also like to thank my fellow LI authors who have willingly answered questions, explained procedures and offered guidance. Thank you to Steve Laube for overseeing my career.

And a big thanks of gratitude to my husband, Bob, for getting up at first-bark and taking care of pets, laundry, grocery shopping, cooking and the countless other things that I neglect because I'm squirreled away in my office.

And finally, "Giving thanks always for all things unto God and the Father in the name of our Lord Jesus Christ" (*Ephesians* 5:20).

# Chapter One

Monday mornings were never easy. Though Hannah King heard her four-year-old son calling, she longed to bury her head under the covers and let her mother take care of him. She'd had a dream about David. It had been so real—David kissing her on their wedding day, David standing beside her as she cradled their newborn son, David moving about the room quietly as he prepared for work.

But he wasn't in the room with her, and he never would be again. A late-summer breeze stirred the window shade. In the distance she could hear the clip-clop of horses on the two-lane, a rooster's crow, the low of a cow. Summer would be over soon. Here in northern Indiana, where she'd grown up, September was met with a full schedule of fall festivals and pumpkin trails and harvest celebrations. She dreaded it all—had no desire to walk through the bright leaves, or decorate with pumpkins or bake apple pies. Fall had been David's favorite time of year. Matthew was born in September. The accident? It had occurred the last week of August. That terrible anniversary was one week away.

This year, the thought of autumn over- whelmed her. Her entire life left her feeling tired and unable to cope. She was happy to be home with her parents, but she hadn't realized the ex- tent of their financial troubles until she'd already moved in. Their church in Wisconsin had used money from the benevolence fund to pay for Matthew's surgeries, but her parents had paid for all of his rehab from their savings. Now they were operating month-to-month, and the stress was beginning to show. She needed to find a job, to help them with the bills, but how could she work when her primary responsibility was to care for Matthew?

She should at least make an attempt to find employment, but she wanted and needed to be home with her son. If she were honest with her- self, she dreaded the thought of interacting with other people on a daily basis. She hadn't enough energy for that.

Hannah pushed off the bedcovers, slipped her feet into a pair of worn house shoes and hurried to the room next door as her mother stepped into the hall.

"I can take care of him if you like."

"*Nein.* I'm awake."

She should have said more, should have thanked her mother, but the memory of David was too heavy on her heart, her emotions too raw. So instead she quickly glanced away and opened the door to Matthew's room.

Though her son was four years old, soon to be five, he still slept in a bed with rails along the side. This was mainly to keep him from falling out.

The thinnest sliver of morning light shone through the gap between the window and the shade, fell across the room and landed on little Matthew. He was lying on his back, his legs splayed out in front of him. Matthew smiled and raised his arms to her, but instead of picking him up, Hannah lowered the wooden rail that her *dat* had fastened to the bed and sat beside him. Matthew struggled to a sitting position and pulled himself into her lap. For a four-year-old, his arms were incredibly strong, probably to make up for the fact that his legs were useless.

"*Gudemariye, Mamm.*" The Pennsylvania Dutch rolled off his tongue, thick with sleep.

"Good morning to you, Matthew."

He reached up and touched her face, patted her cheek, then snuggled in closer.

She gave him a few minutes. Long ago, she'd learned that Matthew needed time to wake up, to adjust to the world. When he was ready, he said, "Potty?"

"Sure thing, Matt."

But before she could pick him up, her father was standing in the doorway. No doubt he'd been awake for hours, and he carried into the room the familiar smells of the barn—hay, horses and even a little manure. It was an earthy smell that Hannah never tired of.

"I thought I heard young Matthew awake."

*"Daddi!"* Matthew squirmed out of her lap and launched himself at her father, who caught him with a smile and carried him into the bathroom across the hall. She could hear them there, laughing and talking about the upcoming day.

Hannah slipped back into her room, changed into a plain gray dress, black apron and white *kapp.* Once dressed, she hurried to the kitchen. If she'd thought she could help her mother make breakfast, she was sadly mistaken.

Steam rose from the platter of fresh biscuits on the table. Another dish held crisp bacon, and her mother was scooping scrambled eggs into a large bowl. Hannah fetched the butter and jam, set them in the middle of the table and then gladly accepted the mug of coffee her mother pushed into her hands.

"Did you sleep well?"

Hannah shrugged, not wanting to talk about it. Then she remembered her bishop's admonition to speak of her feelings more, to resist the urge to let them bottle up inside. Easy enough for him to say. His spouse was still alive and his children did not struggle with a disability. It was an uncharitable thought and added to her guilt.

She sipped the coffee and said, "I fall asleep easily enough, but then I wake after a few hours and can't seem to go back to sleep, no matter how tired I am."

"Normal enough for a woman in mourning."

"It's been nearly a year."

"Grieving takes a different amount of time for different people, Hannah."

"I suppose."

Her mother sat down beside her, reached for her hands.

"Did you have the dream again?"

*"Ya."* Hannah blinked away hot tears. She would not cry before breakfast. She would not. "How did you know?"

Instead of answering, her mother planted a kiss on her forehead, making her feel six instead of twenty-six. Then she popped up and walked back across the kitchen, checking that she hadn't

forgotten anything they might need for breakfast. Holding up the coffeepot, she asked Hannah's father and son, "Coffee for both of you?"

"*Mammi*. I drink milk."

Matthew's laughter lightened the mood. Her
father's steadiness calmed her nerves. Her mother's presence was always a balm to her soul.

The first week she was home, her dad had
insisted on learning how to care for Matthew,
how to help him into his wheelchair. Now Hannah turned to see her father and son, her father standing in the doorway to the kitchen, his
hands on the back of Matthew's wheelchair. Both
looked quite pleased with themselves and ready
to tackle whatever the day might bring.

Jacob Schrock didn't need to hire a driver for
the day's job. Though the Beiler home was technically in a different church district, in reality
they were only a few miles apart. That's the way
things were in Goshen, Indiana. There were so
many Amish that his own district had recently
divided again because they had too many families to fit into one home or barn for church.

Theirs was a good, healthy community. A
growing community.

Which was one of the reasons that Jacob had
plenty of work.

The night before, he'd loaded the tools he

would need into the cargo box fastened on the back of his buggy. The lumber would be delivered to the job site before lunch.

Bo stood stamping his foot and tossing his head as if to ask what was taking so long. Jacob hitched the black gelding to the buggy, glanced back at his house and workshop and then set off down the road. As he directed the horse down Goshen's busy two-lane road, his mind raked back over the letter he'd received from the IRS. How was he going to deal with the upcoming audit and complete the jobs he had contracted at the same time? The accountant he'd contacted had named a quite high hourly rate. The man had also said he'd need a thousand-dollar retainer in order to start the job. Jacob had given serious thought to hiring the accounting firm in spite of their high fees, but in truth he didn't make enough money to afford that.

Jacob had asked around his church, but no one who was qualified had been interested in accounting work. The one young girl who had expressed an interest had quit the first day, and who could blame her? Jacob's idea of filing consisted of giant plastic bins where he tossed receipts.

Jacob loved working for himself, by himself. He'd rather not have anyone in his small office. The bulk of his income came from residential jobs and a few small business contracts, but his heart and soul were invested in building playhouses for children with disabilities. He needed to juggle both, and now, on top of that, he needed to prepare for the audit.

Twenty minutes later he pulled into the Beilers' drive. It wasn't a home he'd ever been to before; that much he was sure of.

Jacob parked the buggy, patted Bo and assured him, "Back in a minute to put you in the field. Be patient." Bo was a fine buggy horse, if a little spirited. Jacob had purchased him six months before. The horse was strong and good-tempered. Unfortunately he was not patient. He'd been known to chew his lead rope, eat anything in sight and paw holes into the ground. He did not handle boredom well.

Grabbing his tool belt and folder with design plans, Jacob hesitated before heading to the front door. This was always the hardest part for him— initially meeting someone. His left hand automatically went to his face, traced the web of scar tissue that stretched from his temple to his chin. He wasn't a prideful man, but neither did he wish to scare anyone.

There was nothing he could do about his appearance, though, so he pulled in a deep breath, said a final word to the horse and hurried to the front door. He knocked, waited and then stood there staring when a young, beautiful woman opened the door. She stood about five and a half feet tall. Chestnut-colored hair peeked out from her *kapp*. It matched her warm brown eyes and the sprinkling of freckles on her cheeks.

There was something familiar about her. He nearly smacked himself on the forehead. Of course she looked familiar, though it had been years since he'd seen her.

"Hannah? Hannah Beiler?"

"Hannah King." She quickly scanned him head to toe. Her gaze darted to the left side of his face and then refocused on his eyes. She frowned and said, "I'm Hannah King."

"But…isn't this the Beiler home?"

"*Ya*. Wait. Aren't you Jacob? Jacob Schrock?"

He nearly laughed at the expression of puzzlement on her face.

"The same, and I'm looking for the Beiler place."

"*Ya*, this is my parents' home, but why are you here?"

"To work." He stared down at the work order as if he could make sense of seeing the first girl he'd ever kissed standing on the doorstep of the place he was supposed to be working.

"I don't understand," he said.

"Neither do I. Who are you looking for?"

"Alton Beiler."

"But that's my father. Why—"

At that point Mr. Beiler joined them, telling Hannah he would take care of their visitor and shaking Jacob's hand. Surely he noticed the scar on Jacob's face, but he didn't dwell on it. "You're at the right house, Jacob. Please, come inside."

"Why would he come inside?" Hannah had crossed her arms and was frowning at him now.

He'd never have guessed when he put on his suspenders that morning that he would be seeing Hannah Beiler before the sun was properly up. The same Hannah Beiler he had once kissed behind the playground and several years later asked out for a buggy ride and dinner. It had been a disastrous date for sure, but still he remembered it with fondness. The question was, what was she doing here?

But then he peered more closely at Alton. Yes, it was Hannah's father for sure and certain. Older, grayer and with wrinkles lining his face, but still her father.

"I haven't seen you in years," Jacob said to Alton.

"Do we know each other?"

"Barely." Jacob chuckled, though Hannah continued to glare at him. "Hannah and I went on a date many years ago."

"It was hardly a date," Hannah chimed in.

"I took you in my buggy."

"Which hadn't been properly cleaned, and your horse was lame."

"I should have checked the horse more carefully."

"We never even made it to dinner."

"I'm surprised you remember."

"And I had to walk home."

"I offered to walk with you."

Hannah rolled her eyes, shook her head and headed back into the house.

"She hasn't changed much," Jacob said in a lower voice.

"Oh, but she has." Alton opened the door wider so that Jacob would come in. "I'm sorry I didn't recognize you."

"It has been ten years."

They passed through a living room that appeared to be sparsely but comfortably furnished. Jacob could smell bacon and biscuits. His stomach grumbled and he instantly regretted that he hadn't taken the time to eat a proper breakfast.

"So your dating Hannah must have been when we were at the other place, on the east side of the district."

"Indeed."

"Obviously we've moved since then." Alton stopped before entering the kitchen, seemed about to say something and then rubbed at the back of his neck and ushered Jacob into the room.

"Claire, maybe you remember Jacob Schrock. Apparently he took our Hannah on a buggy ride once."

Jacob heard them, but his attention was on the young boy sitting at the table. He was young— probably not school-age yet. Brown hair flopped into his eyes and he had the same smattering of freckles as his mother. He sat in a regular kitchen chair, which was slightly higher than the wheelchair parked behind him. No doubt moving back and forth was cumbersome. If he had a small ramp, the chair could be rolled up and locked into place. He should talk to Alton about that. It would be easy enough to create from scrap lumber.

Hannah was helping the child with his breakfast, or perhaps she was merely avoiding Jacob's gaze.

The boy, though, had no problem with staring. He cocked his head to the side, as if trying to puzzle through what he saw of Jacob. Then a smile won out over any questions, and he said, *"Gudemariye."*

"And to you," Jacob replied.

Hannah's mother, Claire, motioned him toward a seat. "Of course I remember you, Jacob. Though you've grown since then."

*"Ya,* I was a bit of a skinny lad." This was the awkward part. He never knew if he should share

the cause of his scars or wait for someone to ask. With the child in the room, perhaps it would be better to wait.

Hannah continued to ignore him, but now the boy was watching him closely, curiously.

"You're taller too, if I remember right. You were definitely not as tall as Alton when you were a *youngie*. Now you're a good six feet, I'd guess."

"Six feet and two inches. My *mamm* used to say I had growth spurts up until I turned twenty." Jacob accepted a mug of coffee and sat down across the table from the boy.

"Who are you?" he asked.

"I'm Jacob. What's your name?"

"Matthew. This is *Mamm*, and that's *Mammi* and *Daddi*. We're a family now." Matthew grinned as if he'd said the most clever thing.

Hannah met Jacob's gaze and blushed, but this time she didn't look away.

"It's really nice to meet you, Matthew. I'm going to be working here for a few days."

"Working on what?"

Jacob glanced at Alton, who nodded once. "I'm going to build you a playhouse."

Hannah heard the conversation going on around her, but she felt as if she'd fallen into the creek and her ears were clogged with water.

She heard it all from a distance. Then Matthew smiled that smile that changed the shape of his eyes. It caused his cheeks to dimple. It was a simple thing that never failed to reach all the way into her heart.

And suddenly Hannah's hearing worked just fine.

"A playhouse? For me?"

"For sure and certain."

"How come?"

Jacob shrugged and waited for Alton to answer the child.

"Some nice people want you to have one."

"Oh. Cool."

"*Dat*, we can't..."

"We most certainly can, Hannah. The charity foundation contacted me last week to make sure it was all right, and I said yes. I think it would be a fine thing for Matthew to have."

"Will I be able to move around in a playhouse? Like, with my wheelchair?"

"You most certainly will," Jacob assured him.

"You're sure?"

"I'm positive."

"Because it don't always fit good. Not in cars or on merry-go-rounds. Sometimes not even in buggies and we have to tie it on the back."

"Your chair will fit in your playhouse. I can promise you that."

Matthew laughed and stabbed his biscuit with his fork, dipped it in a puddle of syrup he'd poured on his plate and stuffed the gooey mess into his mouth.

Hannah's head was spinning. Surely it was a good and gracious thing that someone had commissioned a playhouse for Matthew, but would it be safe for him to play in one? What if he fell out of his chair? What if he rolled out of the playhouse?

How could her father agree to such a thing?

And why was it being built by Jacob Schrock? She hadn't thought about him in years, certainly hadn't expected to see him again. Why today of all days, when her heart was sore from dreaming of David? Why this morning?

"Can I help?" Matthew asked.

"Oh, no." Hannah abandoned her future worries and focused on the problems at hand. "You'll leave that to Jacob."

"But *Mamm…*"

"We can't risk your getting hurt."

"I'll be super careful…"

"And you'd only be in Jacob's way."

Matthew stabbed another piece of biscuit and swirled it into the syrup, but he didn't plop it in his mouth. Instead he stared at the food, worried his bottom lip and hunched up his shoulders. Her son's bullheadedness had been quite useful during his initial recovery. When the doctors had said he probably couldn't do a thing, Matthew had buckled down, concentrated and found a way. There were days, though, when she wondered why *Gotte* had given her such a strong-willed child.

Jacob had drunk half his coffee and accepted a plate of eggs and bacon, which he'd consumed rather quickly. Now he sat rubbing his hand up and down his jaw, his clean-shaven jaw. The right side—the unscarred side. Was the injury the reason he'd never married? Was he embarrassed about the scar? Did women avoid him? Not that it was her business, and she'd certainly never ask.

"I just wanted to help," Matthew muttered.

"Now that you mention it, I could use an apprentice."

"I could be a *'rentice*." Matthew nodded his head so hard his hair flopped forward into his eyes, reminding Hannah that she would need to cut it again soon.

"It's hard work," Jacob cautioned.

"I can work hard."

"You sure?"

"Tell him, *Mamm*. Tell him how hard I work at the center."

"You'd have to hand me nails, tools, that sort of thing."

"I can do that!" Matthew was rocking in his chair now, and Hannah was wise enough to know the battle was lost.

"Only if your *mamm* agrees, of course."

She skewered him with a look. Certainly he knew that he'd backed her into an impossible corner. Instead of arguing, she smiled sweetly and said, "If your *daddi* thinks it's okay."

Hannah's father readily agreed and then Jacob was pulling out sheets of drawings that showed a playhouse in the shape of a train, with extra-wide doors—doors wide enough for Matthew's chair, room to pivot the chair, room to play. How could she not want such a thing for her child? The penciled playhouse looked like the stuff of fairy tales.

When she glanced up at Jacob, he smiled and said in a low voice, "We'll be extra careful."

"I should hope so."

And then she stood and began to clear off the dishes. The last thing she needed to do was stand around staring into Jacob Schrock's deep blue eyes. A better use of her time would be to go to town and pick up the Monday paper so she could study the Help Wanted ads. It looked like that wasn't going to happen. There was no way she was leaving Matthew outside, working as an apprentice to a man who had no children of his own. She'd come home to find he'd nailed his thumb to a piece of wood, or cut himself sawing a piece of lumber, or fallen and cracked something open. Secondary infections were no laughing matter for a child who was a paraplegic.

She'd be spending the morning watching Matthew watch Jacob. As soon as he left for the day, she'd head to town because one way or another, she needed to find a job.

# Chapter Two

Hannah pushed aside her unsettled feelings and worked her way through the morning. She managed to complete the washing and hang it up on the line, and she helped her mother to put lunch on the table, all the while keeping a close eye on what was happening in the backyard.

When it was time for lunch, Matthew came in proclaiming he was an "official 'rentice now," and Jacob followed behind him with a sheepish look on his face.

Her father joined them for the noon meal. Earlier, he had stayed around long enough to confirm where the playhouse would be built and then he'd headed off to the fields. It worried her sometimes, her father being fifty-two and still working behind a team of horses, but her mother only scoffed at that. "What is he supposed to do? Sit in a rocking chair? Your father is as healthy as the bull in the north pasture, and if it's *Gotte's wille*, he'll stay that way for many more years."

The meal had passed pleasantly enough, though Hannah didn't like how enamored Matthew was with Jacob Schrock. They laughed and described their morning's work and talked of trains as if they'd been on one.

"There's a place in town called Tender Jim's." Jacob reached for another helping of potato salad. "Have you heard of it, Matthew?"

Matthew stuffed a potato chip into his mouth and shook his head.

"Down on Danbury Drive. Isn't it?" Her father sat back, holding his glass of tea with one hand and pulling on his beard with the other. "Nice *Englisch* fellow."

"And what were you doing in Tender Jim's?" Claire asked.

"Curious, mostly. I'd taken Dolly to the farrier and had to wait a bit longer than I thought I would. Wandered down and talked to the fellow."

"Did he have trains?" Matthew asked.

"Oh, *ya*. Certainly, he did. Small ones and large ones."

"As large as my playhouse?"

"*Nein.* They were toys."

"Perhaps we could go by and see them sometime," Jacob said.

Hannah jumped up as if she'd been stung by a bee. "Matthew has a full week planned with his physical therapy appointments and all, but *danki* for the offer."

This was exactly why she didn't want a man like Jacob around—or any man for that matter. They'd raise her son's hopes, promise him things they wouldn't deliver and then disappear one day when they realized that Matthew was never going to walk, never going to be normal.

She pretended to be occupied with putting things up in the refrigerator as Jacob, her father and Matthew went out to look at the "job site." Her job was to protect Matthew—from strangers who would pretend to be friends, and from upheaval in his life. Which reminded her that she still hadn't been to town to purchase a newspaper.

She needed to stop worrying, which was easier said than done. Jacob would be finished with the playhouse in a day or two and then Matthew wouldn't see him anymore. Didn't Jacob mention that he was part of a different church district? She hadn't been home long enough to sort the districts out, but she did know there were a lot of Amish in the area. It would explain why she hadn't seen him at church.

Hannah and her mother cleared away the lunch dishes and put together a casserole for dinner and then her mother sat at the table. Hannah continued to peer out the window. What were they doing out there? How could Matthew possibly be helping? Why would Jacob want him to?

"Come sit down a minute, Hannah."

"But—"

"Come on, now. You've been on your feet all morning."

Hannah peeked out the window one last time, then walked to the table and sank into one of the chairs. *Mamm* was putting the finishing touches on a baby quilt for a new mother in their congregation.

Hannah had to force her eyes away from the pastel fabric and the Sunbonnet Sue and Overall Sam pattern. Her mother had given her a similar quilt when Matthew was born. When Hannah had first wrapped her son in that quilt, she'd trusted that only good things would happen in their future. She'd hoped that one day she would wrap her daughter in the same quilt. Now such beliefs didn't come so easily.

"I know you wanted today's paper, but last week's is still next to your father's chair in the sitting room."

"How did you know I wanted a paper?"

"Matthew told me you mentioned it."

Had she told Matthew?

Abandoning any attempt to figure out how

her mother knew things, Hannah fetched a highlighter from a kitchen drawer and the newspaper from the sitting room, folded it open to the Help Wanted section and sat down with a sigh.

"I wish you wouldn't worry about that."

"But we need the money."

"*Gotte* will provide, Hannah."

"Maybe He's providing through one of these ads."

The next twenty minutes passed in silence as Hannah's mood plummeted even lower. The part-time positions paid too little and the full-time positions would require her to be away from home from sunup to sundown, if she could even get one of the positions, which was doubtful since she had no experience. She could always be a waitress at one of the Amish restaurants, but those positions were usually filled by younger girls—girls who hadn't yet married, who had no children.

"He's nice. Don't you think?"

"Who?"

"You know who."

"I don't know who."

"We sound like the owl in the barn."

Hannah smiled at her mother and slapped the newspaper shut. "Okay. I probably know who."

"I guess you were surprised to see him at the door."

"Indeed I was." Hannah should have kept her mouth shut, but she couldn't resist asking, "Do you know what happened to him? To his face?"

"A fire, no doubt." Her mother rocked the needle back and forth, tracing the outline of a Sunbonnet Sue. "We've had several homes destroyed over the years, and always there are injuries. Once or twice the fire was a result of carelessness. I think there was even one caused by lightning."

"A shame," Hannah whispered.

"That he had to endure such pain—yes. I'll agree with that. It doesn't change who he is, though, or his value as a person."

"I never said—"

"You, more than anyone else, should realize that."

"Of course I do."

"You wouldn't want anyone looking at Matthew and seeing a child with a disability. That's not who he is. That's just evidence of something he's endured."

"There's no need to lecture me, *Mamm*."

"Of course there isn't." She rotated the quilt and continued outlining the appliqué. "I can see that Jacob is self-conscious about his scars, though. I hate to think that anyone has been unkind to him."

"His scars don't seem to be affecting Matthew's opinion. He looks at Jacob as if he had raised a barn single-handedly."

"*Gotte* has a funny way of putting people in our life right when we need them."

"I'm not sure this was *Gotte*'s work."

"I know you don't mean that. I raised you to have more faith, Hannah. The last year has been hard, *ya*, I know, but never doubt that *Gotte* is still guiding your life."

Instead of arguing, Hannah opted to pursue a lighter subject. "So *Gotte* sent Jacob to build my son a playhouse?"

"Maybe."

She nearly laughed. Her mother's optimism grated on her nerves at times, but Hannah appreciated and loved her more than she could ever say. *Mamm* had been her port in the storm. Or perhaps *Gotte* had been, and *Mamm* had simply nudged her in the correct direction.

"You have to admit he's easy on the eyes."

"Is that how you older women describe a handsome man?"

"So you think he's *gut*-looking?"

"That's not what I said, *Mamm*."

Claire tied off her thread, popped it through the back of the quilt and then rethreaded her needle. "Tell me about this first date you two had, because I can hardly remember it."

"Small wonder. I was only sixteen."

"*Ya?* Already out of school, then."

"I was. In fact, I was working at the deli counter in town."

"I remember that job. You always brought home the leftover sandwiches."

"Jacob and I attended the same school, in the old district when we lived on Jackspur Lane. He's two years older than me."

"I'm surprised I don't remember your stepping out with him."

"Our house was quite busy then." Hannah was the youngest of three girls. She'd always expected her life to follow their fairy-tale existence. "Beth had just announced her plans to marry Carl, and Sharon was working with the midwife."

"I do remember that summer. I thought things would get easier when you three were out of school, but suddenly I had trouble keeping up with everyone."

"The date with Jacob, it was only my second or third, and I was still expecting something like I read in the romance books."

Her mother tsked.

"They were Christian romance, *Mamm.*"

"I'm guessing your date with Jacob didn't match with what you'd been reading."

"Hardly. First of all, he showed up with mud splattered all over the buggy, and the inside of it was filled with pieces of hay and fast-food wrappers and even a pair of dirty socks."

"Didn't he have older brothers?"

"He had one."

"So I guess they shared the buggy."

Hannah shrugged. "We'd barely made it a quarter mile down the road when we both noticed his horse was limping."

"Oh my."

"It was no big thing. He jumped out of the buggy and began to clean out her hooves with a pick."

"While you waited."

"At first. Then I decided to help, which he told me in no short fashion not to do."

"There are times when it's hard for a man, especially a young man, to accept a woman's help."

"I waited about ten minutes and finally said I was heading home."

"Changed your mind before you were even out of sight of the house."

"Maybe. What I knew for sure was that I didn't want to stand on the side of the road while Jacob Schrock took care of his horse—something he should have done before picking me up."

"Could have been his brother's doing."

"I suppose."

"I hope you didn't judge him harshly because of a dirty buggy and a lame horse."

"Actually, I don't think I judged him at all. I simply realized that I didn't want to spend the evening with him."

"Well, he seems to have turned into a fine young man."

Hannah refolded the newspaper and pointed her highlighter at her mother. "Tell me you are not matchmaking."

"Why would I do such a thing?"

"Exactly."

"Though I did help both of your sisters find their husbands."

"I need a job, *Mamm*. I don't need a husband. I have a son, I have a family and I have a home. I'm fine without Jacob Schrock or any other man." Before her mother could see how rattled she was, Hannah jumped up, stepped over to the window and stared out at Jacob and Matthew.

"At least you parted friends…or so it seems."

Hannah suddenly remembered Jacob kissing her behind the swing set at school. It had been her first kiss, and a bit of a mess. He'd leaned in, a bee had buzzed past her and she'd darted to the right at the last minute. The result was a kiss on the left side of her *kapp*. She'd been mortified, though Jacob had laughed good-naturedly, then reached for her hand and walked her back into the school building. It was three years later when he'd asked her out on the buggy ride.

Remembering the kiss, Hannah felt the heat crawl up her neck. Before her mother could interrogate her further, she busied herself pulling two glasses from the cabinet and said, "Perhaps I should take both of the workers something to drink."

She filled the glasses with lemonade, snagged half a dozen of her mother's oatmeal cookies, put it all on a tray and carried it outside.

After setting it down on the picnic table under the tall maple tree, she turned to watch Jacob and Matthew. In spite of her resolution to maintain a safe distance from Jacob Schrock, her heart tripped a beat at the sight of him.

Which made no sense, because Jacob Schrock was not her type.

He was eight inches taller than she was, whereas David had been her height exactly.

He was blond. David had been dark haired.

His eyes were blue, and David's had been a lovely brown.

Nothing about the man standing near her son appealed to her, least of all the suggestion that he knew what was good for Matthew.

She couldn't help noticing, though...

The sleeves of his blue shirt were rolled up past the elbow, revealing his muscular, tanned arms.

Sweat gleamed on his forehead and caused his blond hair to curl slightly.

As she watched, he handed one end of a tape measure to Matthew, stepped off what was apparently the length of the project and pushed a stake into the ground.

When he was done, Jacob glanced up, noticed her waiting and smiled. Now, why did his smile cause her heart to race even faster? Perhaps she needed to see a doctor. Maybe the depression that had pressed down on her like a dark cloud for so long had finally taken its toll on her heart. Or maybe she was experiencing a normal reaction to a nice-looking man doing a kind deed.

Of course, he was getting paid for it.

But he didn't have to allow Matthew to tag along.

He certainly didn't have to smile at her every time she was near.

Jacob stored the tape measure they were using in a tool belt and said something to Matthew. When her son twisted in his wheelchair to look at her, she had to press her fingers to her lips. Yes, he still sat in his chair, but he looked like a completely different boy. He had rolled up his sleeves, sweat had plastered his hair to his head and a smear of dirt marked his cheek. When he caught her watching, he beamed at her as if it were Christmas Day.

In short, he looked like a normal child having a great time building a playhouse.

Jacob glanced back at Hannah in time to catch her staring at Matthew, the fingers of her right hand pressed against her lips. Jacob considered himself open to beauty. Maybe because of his own disfigurement, he found contentment in noticing *Gotte*'s handiwork elsewhere.

He'd often stood and watched the sunset, thinking that *Gotte* had done a wonderful thing by providing them such splendor. He'd helped his brother when it was time for birthing in the spring: goats, horses, cows, and once when a terrible storm came through and they couldn't get to the hospital—a son. Jacob didn't mind that such things brought him to tears, that he often had to pause and catch his breath, that he was sensitive to the joys of this world.

But when he looked up and saw Hannah, an unfamiliar emotion brushed against the inside of his heart. It couldn't be attraction, as he'd never asked a woman out on a date because of how she looked—not before the fire and not since. He hadn't asked a woman out in years, and he wouldn't be starting today. As for her personality, well, if he were to be honest with himself, she was pushy, obviously overprotective of her son and taciturn to the point of being rude.

She was beautiful, though, and more than that, her obvious love for her son was moving. Her vulnerability in that moment reached deep into his soul and affected him in a way he didn't realize he could be touched.

So he stooped down and said to Matthew, "Best take a break. Your *mamm* has brought us a snack."

He walked beside the boy as they made their way toward the picnic table.

"*Mamm*, I'm helping." Matthew reached for a cookie, broke it in half and stuffed the larger piece into his mouth.

"It appears you worked up an appetite."

Matthew nodded, and Jacob said, "We both did."

Hannah motioned for him to help himself. He popped a whole cookie into his mouth and said, "Wow," before he'd finished chewing. Which caused Matthew to dissolve in a fit of laughter.

"What-id I-ooh?" Jacob asked, exaggerating each syllable.

"You have to chew first," Matthew explained. "And swallow!"

Jacob did as instructed, took a big sip of the lemonade and then said, "*Danki*, Hannah. Hit the spot."

"Looks as if actual construction on this playhouse is slow getting started."

"Measure twice, cut once," Matthew explained.

"We've managed to mark off the dimensions and unload my tools."

"You brought all that lumber in your buggy?"

"*Nein*. The store in town delivered it. I guess you didn't hear the truck."

"I guess I didn't."

"It was this big," Matthew said, holding his arms out wide.

"The playhouse will go up quickly," Jacob assured her. "I'll begin the base of the structure today. The walls will go up tomorrow, and the roof and final details the third day."

"Kind of amazing that a child's toy takes so long to build." Hannah held up a hand and shook her head at the same time. "I did not mean that the way it sounded. It's only that when you consider we can build a barn in one day, it seems funny that a playhouse takes three."

"Sure, *ya*. But this isn't a barn, and, as you can see, young Matthew and I are the only workers."

"I'm going to help," Matthew exclaimed, reaching for another cookie.

Hannah's son was rambling on now, explaining that he could mark the wood before Jacob made the cut and hand him nails as he hammered.

"Wait a minute, Matt. We have therapy tomorrow."

"But—"

"*Nein*. Do not argue with me."

"*Ya*, but this is kind of therapy."

"What time is Matthew's appointment?" Jacob asked, recognizing the escalating disagreement for what it was. Hadn't he argued in the same way when he was a young lad? Maybe not over physical therapy appointments, but there was always something to pull him away from what he'd wanted to do—fishing, searching for frogs, climbing trees.

"Matthew is scheduled for therapy three afternoons a week—Tuesday, Wednesday and Friday."

"That's perfect, because I need help tomorrow morning."

Matthew and Hannah both swiveled to look at him.

"In the afternoon, I'll be doing other stuff that an apprentice isn't allowed to do. But the morning?" Jacob rubbed his hand up and down his jawline as if he needed to carefully consider what he was about to say. Finally he grinned and said, "Mornings will be perfect."

"Yes!" Matthew raised a hand for Jacob to high-five. "I gotta go inside and tell *Mammi*."

Without another word, he reversed the direction of his chair and wheeled toward the house.

"That was kind of you," Hannah said.

"Actually, he is a big help to me."

Instead of arguing, she again pressed her fingers to her lips. Was it so she could keep her emotions inside? Stop her words? Protect her feelings?

"It's only a little thing, Hannah. I'm happy to do it. It's plain to see that Matthew is a special young man."

She picked up the plate of cookies and stared down at it. "He never eats more than one cookie. In fact, he often passes on snacks and desserts. Today he ate two and drank a full glass of lemonade."

"Is that a problem?"

He thought she wouldn't answer. She glanced at him and then her gaze darted out over the area where construction had not yet begun. "The doctors said that the steroids might suppress his appetite, but that it was best to encourage him to eat more."

"And what purpose do the steroids serve?"

"They're supposed to decrease swelling around the spinal cord." She placed the plate on the tray and transferred the empty lemonade glasses to it, as well. "I'm sorry. I didn't mean to bore you with the details."

"Do I look bored?"

She sat on the picnic bench then, staring back toward the house, seemingly lost in her worries over Matthew. "The last thing we needed is him losing weight. Then there are the other complications…"

"Such as?"

"Children with spinal cord injuries often struggle with pneumonia and other breathing disorders. Secondary infections are always a worry—it's why I was afraid for him to help you. If he were to get a cut or take a nasty fall, it could spiral into something worse."

"It must be a lot for you to monitor."

"Matthew needs all his strength, even when it comes in the form of oatmeal cookies."

"I'd like to ask what happened, but I know from personal experience that sometimes you feel like sharing and sometimes you don't."

Hannah jerked her head up. She seemed to study his scars for a moment and then she nodded once. "It's true. Sometimes I want to talk about it, *need* to talk about it, but then other times…"

"I'm listening, if today is one of those days you want to talk."

She pulled in a deep breath and blew it out. "There's not really that much to tell. David and I bought a farm in Wisconsin, after we were married. Life was difficult but *gut*. Matthew came along—a healthy baby boy. My husband was out harvesting, and Matthew was riding up on the bench seat with him. This was a year ago…one year next week."

"What happened?"

"There was a snake coiled in the grass. The work horse nearly stepped on it. He reared up, throwing both David and Matthew. David was killed instantly when the harvester rolled over him. I suppose because he was smaller, Matthew was thrown farther. Otherwise he would have been killed, as well."

"Instead he was injured."

"He suffered a complete spinal cord break."

"I'm so sorry."

Jacob allowed silence to fill the hurting places between them. Finally he asked, "Surgeries?"

"*Ya*—two. The first was for the initial diagnosis, to evaluate and stabilize the fractured backbone. The second was a follow-up to the first."

"And you had to handle it all alone."

"Of course I didn't." Now her chin came up and when she glanced at him, Jacob saw the old stubbornness in her eyes. "My church helped me, my sister came to stay awhile and then… then my parents suggested I move home."

"Family is *gut*."

"*Ya*, it is, except that our being here is a drain on them."

Jacob was unsure how to answer that. He didn't know Claire or Alton Beiler well, but he was certain they didn't consider Hannah and Matthew to be a drain. It was plain from the way they interacted that they wanted their daughter and grandson at home with them.

"I'm happy to have Matthew working with me, Hannah, but only if it's okay with you. I promise to be very careful around him."

She didn't answer. Instead she nodded once, gathered up the tray and followed her son into the house.

Leaving Jacob standing in the afternoon sunshine, wondering what else he could do to lighten the burden she carried, wondering why it suddenly seemed so important for him to do so.

He needed to stay focused on his business, on making enough money to pay an accountant before the audit was due, on the other playhouses he would build after this. But instead, as he went back to work, he found himself thinking of a young boy with dirt smeared across his nose and a beautiful mother who was determined to keep others at arm's length.

# Chapter Three

Hannah was grateful that she was busy the next morning. Maybe it would take her mind off of finding a job, which was becoming all she thought about. She'd spent an hour before breakfast going over the Help Wanted ads once again, but nothing new had appeared. There wasn't a single listing that she felt qualified to do, and she doubted seriously that anything new had been listed in the last few days. So instead of obsessing over what she couldn't change, she focused on helping her mother.

Tuesday was baking day. They mixed bread, kneaded dough, baked cookies and prepared two cakes. The kitchen was hot and steamy by the time they were finished. Her mother sank into a chair and said, "You're a big help, Hannah. I wouldn't want to do all of this alone."

Of course, she wouldn't need so much if they weren't there.

And Hannah knew that her mother rarely baked alone. Most weeks her niece Naomi came over to help. Still, the compliment lightened her heart as she called to Matthew. She'd helped him change into clean clothes after lunch, and he had promised not to get dirty. Now he was sitting in his chair, watching out the window as Jacob raised the walls of his playhouse.

"Looks like a real train, huh?" her mother asked.

Hannah cocked her head left and then right. "Can't say as it does."

"To me it's plain as day."

"Which is all that matters." She reached out and mussed her son's hair. "We should get going so we won't be late."

They made it to the PT center in downtown Goshen twenty minutes before their appointment. For the next two hours, Hannah sat in the waiting room and crocheted, or attempted to. Her mind kept wandering and she'd find that she'd dropped a stitch and then she would have to pull out the row and start over. After an hour, she'd made very little progress on the blue shawl, so she decided to put it away and flip through some of the magazines.

The center served both Amish and *Englisch*,

so the magazine selection was varied. There were copies of the *Budget*, but there were also copies of *National Geographic*, *Home & Garden* and even *People* magazine.

She reached for *Home & Garden*.

On the cover was a picture of a sprawling country home, with flowers blooming along the brick pavement that bordered the front of the house. Orange, yellow and maroon mums filled containers on the porch. Pink begonias hung from planters on either side of the door.

"It would be nice if life were like those pictures." Sally Lapp sat down beside her with a *harrumph* and a sigh. Sally was plump, gray and kind.

"How's Leroy?"

"*Gut.* I suppose. Ornery, if I were to be honest."

Sally reached into her bag and pulled out a giant ball of purple yarn and two knitting needles. She'd shared the previous week that she was expecting her forty-second grandchild, and they were all sure it would be a girl. If by some strange twist of fate it was a boy, she'd save the blanket for an auction and knit another in an appropriate shade of green or blue.

"Is Leroy able to get around any better?" Hannah asked.

"Old coot tried to move from the living room

to the bedroom by himself, without his walker. I was outside harvesting some of the garden vegetables when he fell." She glanced over her cheater glasses at Hannah, but never slowed in her knitting. "Fell, bruised his hip and scared a year of life off of me."

"I'm so sorry."

"Not your fault, child. How's young Matthew?"

*"Gut."* Hannah flipped through the magazine, too quickly to actually see anything on the pages.

"There's more you're not saying, which is fine. Some things we need to keep private, but take it from me—it's best to share when something is bothering you. Share with someone you can trust not to shout it to the nearest *Budget* scribe."

Hannah considered that for a moment. Maybe it would help to share her worries, especially with someone outside the family, and she could trust Sally to keep anything she said confidential.

"The Sunshine Foundation purchased supplies for a playhouse for Matthew—a special one, you know. It will have handicap rails and all."

"What a *wunderbaar* thing."

"And the National Spinal Cord Injury Association hired someone to build it."

"Even better. I know your father is very busy with his crops."

"Jacob Schrock showed up yesterday—to build the playhouse, which is in the shape of a train. I'm afraid that Matthew is fairly smitten with him."

Sally glanced at her once, but she didn't offer an opinion. She continued knitting, as if she were waiting for Hannah to say more. But Hannah didn't know what else to say. She didn't know why it bothered her so much that Matthew liked Jacob.

"I suppose I'm worried is all. I know Jacob will be done in a few days and then...most likely... Matthew won't see him anymore. I've tried to explain this, but Matthew doesn't listen. He prattles on about how he's Jacob's apprentice."

"It's natural for young boys Matthew's age to look up to their elders—your father, your brothers-in-law, the men in church."

"*Ya.* I know it is. But those are all people who are a constant presence in his life."

"Soon he will be in school," Sally continued. "I'm sure you realize that some teachers stay a long time, but others only last a year."

"I hadn't thought of that."

"Some people are in our lives permanently. Others? *Gotte* brings them to us for a short time."

Instead of answering, Hannah sighed.

Sally turned the baby blanket and began a row of purl stitches. They flowed seamlessly together with the knit stitches. The result was a pattern that looked as if it had been produced in an *Englisch* factory.

"Jacob Schrock, he's a *gut* man."

"Is he in your district?"

"He was, but we had to split recently. So many families. So many *grandkinner*."

"I went to school with him, but that was years ago."

"Before his accident, then."

*"Ya."* Hannah pulled the shawl she was supposed to be working on back out of her bag, but she didn't bother with hunting for the crochet needle.

"Terrible thing. Both of his parents were killed. The fire chief said the blaze was caused by a lightning strike. Jacob was out in the buggy when it happened. I heard that he saw the blaze from the road, ran into the burning house, and pulled out his *mamm* and his *dat*, but it was too late."

Hannah's hand went to her left cheek. "That's how he got the scars?"

"For sure and certain. He was in the hospital for a long time. The doctors wanted to do more surgeries…graft skin onto his face. They said that he would look as *gut* as new."

"So why didn't they?"

Sally shrugged. "He would still be a man who had lost his parents in a fire, who had endured unfathomable pain. Removing the scars from his face wouldn't have removed the scars from his heart."

"Yes, but—"

"Jacob decided not to have the additional surgeries. Our bishop would have allowed it, but Jacob said no. He said the money that had been donated should go to someone else."

"Kind of him."

"*Ya*, he is a kind man. He was also very depressed for…" Sally stared across the room, as if she were trying to count the years, to tally them into something that made sense. "For two, maybe three years. Rarely came to church. Kind of hid inside his house."

"What changed?" Hannah asked. "When did he start making playhouses?"

"I suppose the playhouse building started a few years ago. As to what changed, you'd have to ask Jacob."

"He seems happy enough now."

"Trouble finds us all from time to time. Now Jacob is dealing with this tax audit."

"Tax audit?"

"They're not saying he did anything wrong,

mind you. Only that he'll have to produce ledgers and receipts."

"Can he?"

Sally grimaced as she again turned the blanket and began a new row of knit stitches. "My granddaughter tried to work for him. She lasted less than a day. Said that he'd apparently been paying his taxes based on some system he kept scribbled on random sheets of paper. Said she couldn't make any sense of it at all."

"Oh my."

"And the receipts? Thrown into bins with the year taped on the outside. A giant mess according to Abigail. Said she'd rather keep waitressing than deal with that. Fortunately, she was able to get her old job back."

"But what about Jacob?"

"He's still looking for someone." Sally's needles stopped suddenly, clicking together as she dropped them in her lap. "Seems I remember you being very *gut* in math."

"That was years ago."

"It's an ability, though, not something you forget."

"I wouldn't—"

"And didn't you mention last week that you were worried about your parents' finances?"

"Well, yes, but… I'm looking for a job that pays well, something in town perhaps."

"Any success?"

"Not yet."

Sally picked up her needles again, and Hannah hoped the subject was dropped. She could not work for Jacob Schrock. He would be out of her life by the end of the week. The last thing she needed was to be in constant contact with him, working with him on a daily basis. The way he looked at her? Such a mixture of pity and compassion. She didn't need to face that every day, and how could she leave Matthew?

Always her mind circled back to that final question. How could she leave her son eight, maybe even nine hours a day? Could she expect her mother to pick up the slack? How was *Mamm* supposed to cope with one more thing on top of all she had to do?

Matthew wheeled through the doorway and into the waiting room, a smiley sticker on the back of his hand, and Hannah began gathering up her things. It was as she turned to go that Sally said, "Think about it, Hannah. It could be that you would be a real blessing to Jacob, and maybe…maybe it would solve your problems in the process."

She'd have to ask Jacob about the job.

Only of course, she wouldn't. It was all none of her business. Soon he'd be done with the playhouse and she wouldn't see him again, which would suit her just fine. Dolly clip-clopped down the road, more content with the day than Hannah was.

She would be content, if she had a job. If they didn't have financial problems. If she wasn't so worried about Matthew.

It would be crazy to consider working for Jacob.

He might be a kind, talented man, but he was also damaged. He'd suffered a terrible loss, which might explain why he pushed his nose into other people's business. Just the day before, he'd looked at her as if she was crazy when she'd tried to put a sweater on Matthew. True, it was eighty degrees, but Matthew had been known to catch a cold in warmer weather than that.

Nope. Jacob Schrock didn't belong in her life.

Matthew peeled the sticker off his hand and stuck it on to the buggy.

"Your therapists said you did a *gut* job today."

"Uh-huh."

"They also said you did everything fast, that you seemed to be in a rush to be done."

"Are we almost home?"

"A few more miles."

"Faster, please."

"You want me to hurry this old buggy mare?"

"*Daddi*'s horse is faster."

"Indeed." Her father had ordered a second buggy horse when she'd come home to live. Hannah had protested it wasn't necessary, but he'd insisted. Come to think of it, maybe he'd insisted because Dolly was getting older and they'd have to replace her soon, which didn't bear thinking about. Dolly was the first buggy horse that Hannah had learned to drive.

While Matthew stared out the window, he pinched his bottom lip in between his thumb and forefinger, pulling it out like a pout and then letting it go. It was a habit that she saw only when he was anxious about something.

And she didn't doubt for a minute that the source of his anxiety was right now hammering two-by-fours into the shape of a train.

They were about to pass the parking area for the Pumpkinvine Trail. Hannah pulled on the right rein and called out to Dolly, who docilely turned off the road.

"Why are we stopping?" Matthew frowned out at the trail, a place he usually enjoyed visiting.

"We need to talk."

Now he stared up at her, eyes wide. "Am I in trouble?"

"No, Matt. Not at all."

"Then what?"

Instead of answering, she studied him a minute. Already he had such a unique personality—with his own likes, dislikes and ideas. Admittedly, she felt more protective of him than most mothers might feel of a nearly five-year-old child, but she understood that this concern wasn't only about his disability. It was also about his not having a father, about his missing the presence of a dad in his life.

"You like Jacob a lot. Don't you?"

"Yes!"

"But you remember that he's only at our house because some people paid him to be there."

"Uh-huh."

"He's doing a job."

"And I'm his *'rentice*."

Hannah sighed, closed her eyes, and prayed for patience and wisdom. When she opened her eyes, Matt reached out and patted her hand. "Don't worry, *Mamm*. He's a *gut* guy. Even *Daddi* said so."

"Oh, *ya*, I'm sure he is."

"So what's wrong?"

"Nothing's wrong, really. But you do understand that Jacob is only going to be at our house for a few days, right? Then he'll have another job, building another playhouse for someone else."

Matt frowned and pulled on his bottom lip. "Another kid like me?"

"I don't know."

"Okay."

"Okay?" Hannah reached out and brushed the hair out of his eyes.

"Uh-huh."

"What do you mean, okay?"

"It's okay that Jacob won't be at our house because he'll be at somebody else's house making them happy."

Since she didn't have an answer for that, she called out to Dolly, who backed up and then trotted out of the parking area, back onto the two-lane.

She was willing to admit that possibly her son saw things more clearly than she did. Didn't the Bible tell them they were to become like little children? Hannah wasn't sure she'd be able to do that—her worries weighed too heavily on her heart, but maybe in this situation she could follow Matt's lead. At least for a few more days.

And she would double her efforts looking for a job because she most certainly was not going to ask Jacob about what kind of help he needed.

Jacob had always enjoyed working on playhouses. He liked building things with an eye for small children. Some people might say it was because his own father had built him a similar type of playhouse. But his father had also taught him to play baseball and he had no urge to coach the *youngies*. His father had taught him how to sow seed and harvest it, but he had no desire to be a farmer.

He was grateful for his father, for both of his parents, and he still missed them terribly. But learning to build wooden playthings for children had been a gift from *Gotte*, a real blessing at the lowest point in his life. Today he was able to share part of that blessing with young Matthew, and he wanted every piece of it to be as good as he could make it.

So he measured everything twice—the main doorway into the train, the back door which ended on a small porch and the entryways between the cars. Wheelchairs required extra room and Matthew would probably require a larger chair as he grew. Though he was nearly five now, children as old as ten or even twelve often played on the structures that Jacob made. As Matthew grew, no doubt his chair would become a bit bigger. Jacob wanted the playhouse to be as accessible to him as his home.

He sanded the floor smoothly so that the wheels of the chair wouldn't hang up on an uneven board.

He added a little extra height so that Matthew's friends who would be standing and walking and running could play along beside him.

And when he heard the clatter of a buggy, he put down his tools and ambled over to meet Hannah and Matthew.

"Hi, Jacob. I can help now."

"You already helped me this morning. Remember?"

"*Ya*, but—"

"Actually I'm about to call it a day."

"Oh."

"There is one thing I need...won't take but a minute."

"Sure! Anything. What is it?"

"I need you to come and do an early inspection."

"You do?"

"Yup. I need my apprentice's opinion before I move forward."

"Cool!"

Hannah had parked the buggy, set the brake and jogged around to help Matthew out.

Jacob stepped forward as if to help, but a frown from Hannah and a short shake of her head convinced him not to try. She was obviously used to doing things on her own. So instead he stood there, feeling like an idiot because a woman weighing roughly the same as a hundred pound sack of feed struggled with simply helping her son out of a buggy.

As he watched, she removed the straps that

secured the wheelchair to the back of the buggy, then set it on the ground, opened it, secured something along the back. Finally she opened the buggy's door wide so that Matthew's legs wouldn't bang against anything.

"Ready?" she asked.

"Ready." He threw his arms around her neck and she stepped back as she took the full weight of him, then settled him into the chair.

How would she do this when he was seven or ten or twelve? How would Hannah handle the logistics of a fully grown disabled son? Was there any possibility that he would ever regain the use of his legs? Jacob had a dozen questions, and he didn't ask any of them because it wasn't really his business.

He reached into the buggy, snagged Matt's straw hat and placed it on his head. The boy gave him a thumbs-up, and adjusted himself in the chair as easily as Jacob straightened his suspenders in the morning.

"Let's go," Matthew said.

"Whoa. Hang on a minute. We need to see to your *mamm*'s horse first."

"I can take care of Dolly," Hannah insisted.

"Nonsense." He stepped closer to Hannah and lowered his voice. "What kind of neighbor would I be if I let you do that?"

"You're our neighbor now?"

"In a sense."

"So you want to take care of my horse?"

"*Ya.* I do."

"Fine. I'll just go inside and have a cup of tea."

"But I thought you might go with us and…" His words slid away as she walked toward the house, waving without turning around.

"Come on, Jacob. Let's do this."

Matthew wheeled alongside him as he led the mare into the barn.

"Her name's Dolly," Matthew said when they stopped inside the barn.

The horse lowered her head so that she was even with the boy. Matthew sat in front of her and stroked from her forehead to her muzzle.

"Good Dolly," Matthew said.

Jacob unhitched the buggy, took off the harness and placed it on the peg on the wall, and then led Dolly through the barn to the pasture.

"Now?" Matt asked.

"Now."

Matt had to move slowly over the parts of uneven ground that led to where the playhouse was being constructed. It was definitely the best place for the structure, as Alton had noted. But the going was a little rough, and it occurred to Jacob that a wooden walk would make things much easier. He had enough lumber scraps at home to do it. An extra day, maybe two, and he could have a nice smooth path from the driveway to the playhouse.

"That is way cool," Matt exclaimed, sounding exactly like an *Englisch* boy Jacob had built a playhouse for the week before. Kids were kids, and *cool* was a pretty standard response to something they liked.

"Let's show you the inside."

Jacob let Matthew go first and watched as he maneuvered his way up the small ramp and into the main cabin of the train. The engine room was to his left and the passenger car was to his right. Beyond that was a small back porch. On an actual train, this would be the end of the observation car, and the area would resemble a roofed porch. Now that he thought about it, a roof wasn't a bad idea. He could add it easily enough.

Matthew made his way to the front of the train. Jacob had created a space where he could pull up his wheelchair and pretend he was in the conductor's seat. To his right Jacob had fastened a wooden bench and in front of him there were knobs and such for him to pull and pretend to direct the train.

"Wow," he said.

"We're not finished yet, buddy. We still need to put on the roof, and…other stuff."

"Can I help?"

"I'm counting on it. I'll be here early tomorrow morning."

They were standing right next to each other, or rather, Jacob was standing next to Matthew. Before Jacob realized what was happening, Matt had pivoted in his seat and thrown his arms around his legs.

*"Danki,"* the boy said in a low voice.

*"Ger gschehne."* Jacob found that his voice was tight, but the words of their ancestors passed between them as easily as water down a riverbed.

Jacob pushed Matthew's chair the length of the car. They moved slowly, studying every detail, until Hannah's *mamm* came outside and rang the dinner bell.

Jacob did not intend to stay and eat, but it seemed that Claire expected it. She'd already set an extra place at the table. It would have been rude to refuse, or so he told himself.

The meal was satisfying and the conversation interesting. He realized that too often he ate alone, that he actually missed the back-and-forth between family members. There was no reason for it either. His brother lived next door, and he had a standing offer to eat with them.

Why had he pulled away?

Had it been so painful to see what he would never have?

There was no such awkwardness with Hannah's family. Claire spoke of the painted bunting she'd spied on the birdbath. Alton updated them on the crops. Hannah described how well Matthew had done at physical therapy.

As for Matthew, he was practically nodding off in his seat by the time they'd finished eating.

Hannah excused herself, transferred him from the dinner chair to the wheelchair and pushed him down the hall.

"She's pretty amazing, your daughter." He hadn't meant to say the words. They'd slipped from his heart to his lips without consulting his brain.

If Alton and Claire were surprised, they hid it well. Claire stood and began clearing the table. Alton offered to see him out. They'd stepped outside when Jacob shared his ideas for a wooden walk to the playhouse as well as a small platform for the dinner table.

"Must be hard on Hannah, on her back I mean—moving him from one chair to the other so often."

"And I have to be fast to beat her to it. Your ideas sound *gut*, but I'm afraid the grant doesn't cover that, and I don't have any extra money at the moment."

Jacob waved away his concerns. "I have leftover lumber. It won't cost me anything but time."

"Which is precious for every man."

"It's okay. I don't have to start the next job until Monday." He didn't mention the orders he had at his shop. He could put in a few hours each night and stay ahead on that.

"Then I accept, and I thank you."

"You can tell me it's none of my business, but Hannah seemed particularly preoccupied tonight. Is something wrong? Something else?"

Alton stuck his thumbs under his suspenders. "Money is a bit tight."

"How tight?"

"Missed a few payments on the place."

"What did your banker say about that?"

"Said they could extend me another thirty days, but then they'll have to start the foreclosure process."

"I'm sorry, Alton. I had no idea. Have you spoken to your bishop?"

Alton waved that idea away. "My family has received plenty of help from the benevolence fund in the last year. We'll find a way through this on our own."

"And Hannah?"

"Hannah is determined to find a job."

The entire drive home he thought of Alton's words, of the family's financial problems and of the help he needed in order to prepare him for the IRS audit. He could ask Hannah. It wasn't a completely crazy idea. He remembered that she was good at sums, and it wasn't as if she needed to understand algebra. It only required someone more organized than he was.

She was stubborn and willful and curt at times, but he wasn't going to be dating her. He was going to hire her.

Or was he?

It wasn't until he was home and cleaning up for bed that he realized the error of his thinking. He caught sight of his reflection in the small bathroom mirror and stared for a moment at his scars. His fingers traced the tissue that was puckered and discolored. He'd been so fortunate that his eye wasn't permanently damaged, and in truth he'd become used to the sight of his charred, disfigured flesh.

Others, though, they often found his face harder to look at. They would turn away, or blush bright red and hurry off. Sometimes children cried when they first saw him.

Had he forgotten about those reactions?

Did he really think that his appearance wouldn't matter to a woman, to an employee? Hannah had been polite, sure, but that didn't mean that she wasn't horrified by the sight of his scars.

As for the thought of her working with him,

she probably wouldn't want to spend her days in the company of a disfigured man. Possibly he even reminded her of the accident that had killed her husband. He would be a constant reminder of her misfortune.

He'd been around her for two days, and he was already creating sandcastles in the sky. Probably because he'd felt an instant connection to her and that was okay and proper. As a friend. As a brother. But what about as an employer?

He hadn't spent much time around women in the last few years. It was simply easier not to. Sure, he knew what he was missing out on, but it wasn't as if he had a chance with any of the single girls in their district. Even the widows could do better than him. He might have grown comfortable with his disfigurement, but he wouldn't ask that of a woman.

But he wasn't thinking about courting. He was thinking about a business arrangement, which was crazy. He'd seen the look of relief pass over her features when he'd promised her he would be done this week. She was already looking forward to having him out of their lives. Why would he offer her a job?

On top of which, she'd had enough tragedy in her life. He wouldn't be adding to that burden with his own problems. No, she'd be better off working in town, working for an *Englisch* shop owner. He'd do best to keep his distance. As for the audit, perhaps he could scrape up enough money for the accounting firm. He'd need to do something and do it quick, because the clock was ticking down to his deadline. Not that he remembered it exactly, but it was within the next month. That much he knew for certain.

Four weeks, maybe a little less.

By then, he needed to have found a solution.

# Chapter Four

Hannah had scoured the paper on both Wednesday and Thursday looking for a job. What she found was discouraging. The Amish restaurant in town wanted her to work the four-to-nine shift. She wouldn't be home to share the evening meal or put Matthew to bed. The thought caused her stomach to twist into a knot.

Amish Acres in Nappanee needed someone in the gift shop, and they understood that Amish employees didn't work on Sundays. They even provided a bus that picked up workers in downtown Goshen for the twenty-minute ride. But she would be required to work on Saturday. In an Amish household, Saturday was a day spent preparing for Sunday—cooking meals, cleaning the house, making sure clothes were cleaned and pressed. She wouldn't be able to do any of that if she worked at Amish Acres.

And with any of the jobs she considered, the same questions lingered in the back of her mind. Who would take Matthew to his physical therapy appointments during the week? Could she really expect her mother to add one more thing to her already full schedule? Could her mother handle the physical demands of lifting Matthew in and out of the buggy?

She studied the local paper once more Friday morning, in between helping her mother with the meals and taking care of Matthew. After lunch, she again donned a fresh apron and set off to take Matthew to his appointment. She had an interview for a job late that afternoon, and her father had offered to meet them in town.

"You didn't have to do this," she said as she helped Matthew into the other buggy.

"I like riding with *Daddi*," Matthew piped up. "He drives faster than you do."

"I could have…"

"What? Taken him with you? *Nein*. It's not a problem. My order had come in at the feed store, and young Matthew can help check off items as they load them in the back of my buggy. Besides, I know this interview is important to you."

"Yes, but it's not for another hour. I could have brought him home."

"Go and order yourself a nice cup of tea at

that bakery." Her father had clumsily patted her arm and then turned his attention to Matthew.

"Ready, Matt?"

"More than ready. Is Jacob done with the playhouse yet? Is he still there? Because I made him a drawing. I need to give it to him."

Hannah didn't hear the rest of the conversation as they pulled away. She didn't have to hear it to know what Matthew was saying. He'd been talking about the playhouse and Jacob all week.

She, on the other hand, had specifically avoided Jacob that morning. The more she thought about the job opening he had, the more irritated she grew. He definitely knew that her family was in a tough financial situation. She'd heard her father talking to him about it. Why hadn't he offered her the job?

Did he think she wasn't smart enough to handle a column of numbers?

Did he worry that she wouldn't be a good employee?

Or maybe—and this was the thing that pricked her heart—maybe he would be happy to be free of her and Matthew. Building a playhouse for a week was one thing. Involving yourself in someone's life, especially when that someone had special needs, was another thing completely.

Hannah's interview was at the new craft store in town. The ad said they were looking for an experienced quilter. That was one thing Hannah was quite good at, but then wasn't every Amish woman? Still, if it was the job she was meant to have, *Gotte* would provide a way.

She arrived early and carefully filled out the employment questionnaire, balancing the piece of paper on her lap with only a magazine under it for support. When she had finished, the cashier had taken it from her and told her to wait. The young girl had returned twenty minutes later and led her into a back office.

The owner of the shop was in her forties, stylishly dressed, sporting short black hair, dangly earrings and bright red fingernails.

She stared at the questionnaire for a moment and then she asked, "Do you wear your bonnet every day?"

"Excuse me?"

"Your…" The woman touched the top of her head.

"It's a prayer *kapp*, and *ya* we always wear it when we are out in public."

"Oh, good. I think the customers will like that, and your clothing—it's so quaint, so authentic. Wouldn't want you showing up in jeans and a T-shirt."

"I don't own any jeans."

"It would also be helpful if you'd park your buggy out front so that tourists can see it."

"There's no shade out front, and I wouldn't want Dolly to stand on the concrete pavement all day."

"I see." The woman pursed her too-red lips and steepled her fingers. "I'm sure we can work something out. Also, we'd like you to speak as much German…"

"Pennsylvania Dutch," Hannah corrected her softly.

"Excuse me?"

"We speak Pennsylvania Dutch and *Englisch*, of course."

"Yes, but that's the thing. I'd rather you speak your language." The woman sat back and rocked slightly in her leather office chair. "I know you people aren't particularly business savvy, but this is a big venture for my executive board. We have stores in Ohio and Pennsylvania, but this is our first in Indiana. I intend for it to be the best."

"Which means what, exactly?"

"Tourists come here to catch a glimpse into a different life, to experience in some small way what it means to be different."

"I'm different?"

"We don't want to minimize that—we want to showcase it. We'll be selling the experience of meeting an Amish person as much as we're selling fabric."

"Selling?"

"And didn't you mention on your form that your son…"

"Matthew."

"Isn't he disabled? If you could bring him in with you, just now and then when he'd be in town anyway, I think that would be a real plus."

"Bring Matthew in for *Englischers* to gawk at?"

But the woman wasn't listening. She'd already opened a file and was flipping through sheets of paper. "How would you feel about appearing on the flyers that we're going to place around town? You're young enough, and if we added just a touch of makeup I think you'd photograph well."

The muscles in Hannah's right arm began to quiver and a terrible heat flushed through her body. She hadn't been this angry since…well, ever. Knowing she was about to say something unkind, Hannah gathered up her purse, politely thanked the woman and rushed from the store.

Once she made it back outside, she stood beside Dolly, running her hand down the horse's neck and breathing in the scent of her. Slowly the tide of anger receded, and she was left shaking her head in amazement. How could a person be so insensitive? How could she think that such tactics were acceptable? Hannah would not allow herself or her son to be put on display. What was the woman thinking? Only of her business, of making a profit, of selling the Amish experience.

Hannah understood that tourism was a big part of the Goshen economy. It benefited both *Englisch* and Amish, and there were many places that treated Plain folks with respect. Meeting people from other states was fun for both parties, and the added income was often a big help to families. But she would not be wearing makeup or putting her son and horse on display for anyone.

She would not be working for the new craft shop in town.

Jacob looked up as Hannah pulled into the drive. He'd been watching for her. He'd actually finished the job a few hours ago, and now he was looking for things to do until she came home. Since they didn't attend the same church, it would be his last time to see her unless they happened to run into one another in town or at a wedding or funeral.

Hannah practically jumped out of the buggy and didn't so much as glance his way.

Was it possible that she was unhappy with what he'd done?

Jacob turned and surveyed the play area. The train playhouse was complete, and if he allowed himself to think about it, the finished structure looked better than he'd imagined. The board-walk leading to it was smooth and wide enough for Matthew's wheelchair.

But the crowning jewel of the project wasn't the structure itself but the boy he'd built it for. Matthew was sitting in the front engine room, a train conductor's hat perched jauntily on his head as he tooted the horn and spoke to his imaginary passengers and crew. The young boy had quite an imagination, and he was enthusi-astically happy with the new playhouse. Jacob closed his eyes, prayed that *Gotte* would bless young Matthew, and his family—his grand-parents, his aunts and uncles, and of course his mother.

He'd no sooner thought of Hannah than she appeared before him, clutching an envelope in her hand.

"Hire me to work in your office."

"Excuse me?"

"Sally Lapp says you're looking for someone."

"*Ya*, I am."

"So why haven't you offered the job to me?" She took a step closer and Jacob took a step back.

"I didn't think—"

"Didn't think I could handle it?"

"Of course you can, but—"

"I beat your class at math drills even though you were two years older."

"I remember."

"And I have experience in accounting. I did some before Matthew was born."

"That's *gut*, but—"

She waved the envelope in front of his face so that he had to step back again or risk being swiped by it.

"Do you know what this is? A notice from the bank. *Dat* has less than a month to come up with his back payments. If he doesn't, they'll begin the foreclosure process."

"I'm sorry to hear that."

"While you were out here building a play-house my parents stand to lose their farm."

"The playhouse didn't—"

"Didn't cost them anything? *Ya*, I know. But we do. Matthew and I do. There's the extra food and the clothing and Matthew's medical expenses…" Her eyes shone brightly with tears, and she quickly pivoted away.

He gave her a moment—counted to three and then did so again. Finally he stepped forward and said, "I'd be pleased to have you work in my office. I didn't ask because I wasn't sure you'd want such a challenge."

He couldn't bring himself to admit that he didn't think she'd want to be around him, that his scars might repulse her or even remind her of Matthew's accident.

"You don't think I'm up to it, do you?" The fire was back—softer, simmering this time.

"I don't doubt your bookkeeping skills, Hannah. However, I'm not sure you realize how terrible I am at filing and record keeping."

Hannah waved that away. "I know all about that. I even know you had one girl quit after only a day."

"And I didn't blame her."

"So what did you plan to do?"

"About?"

"About the IRS audit." Hannah squinted up at him quizzically, waiting to hear what his plan was. Only Jacob didn't have a plan.

"I still have almost three weeks. I figured… well, I figured it would work itself out somehow."

"That's not a plan."

"You've got me there."

"Is this a permanent position?"

"I haven't really thought about it."

"Why am I not surprised?"

"It could be, I guess. Don't know how much work there would be once the records are straightened out. I guess we could get past the audit and then decide."

Hannah crossed her arms and studied the

playhouse, really saw it for maybe the first time since he'd begun construction. "It's a *gut* playhouse."

"*Ya*, it is."

"Matthew loves it."

"He's a great kid."

"*Danki*."

"*Ger gschehne*." And there it was, a tangible bond between them—the ways of their parents and grandparents, the river of their past that set them apart and also drew them together.

"I'll start Monday," she said and then she named what she expected to make per hour.

Jacob almost laughed. He would readily pay more if she was able to get him out of the paperwork jam he'd created, but instead of offering more he simply nodded. Perhaps he could give her a bonus once the audit was complete.

Hannah's eyebrows rose in surprise that he'd agreed, but she was holding something back. She was chewing on her thumbnail, a habit they'd all teased her about in school. The memory blossomed in Jacob's mind with the force of a winter wind—Hannah standing at the board, worrying her thumbnail as she worked out some impossibly difficult math problem. At least it had seemed impossible to him.

"What is it?" he asked, the question coming

out more gruffly than he'd intended. "What's worrying you?"

She stood straighter, glanced at her son and then looked back at Jacob. "I'll need to take off during Matthew's appointments."

"Of course."

"So you wouldn't...you wouldn't mind?"

"*Nein.* Your son's therapy is important. I would be a fool not to understand that."

She nodded once, and then she stuck the offending envelope from the bank in her apron pocket and went to her son. She climbed the steps and sat beside him in the engine room, leaving Jacob to enjoy the sight of them and the sound of their laughter as Matthew set his conductor cap on her head.

"We were hoping Jacob would stay for dinner."

Hannah's mother set the large pot of chicken and dumplings in the middle of the table. Beside it was a loaf of fresh bread, butter and a large bowl with a salad that Hannah had managed to throw together.

"He told me he has a mess at home to clean up." Matthew slathered butter on top of his piece of bread and took a large bite. When he caught Hannah staring at him, he smiled broadly.

Her father spoke of the rain forecast for the next week. Her mother had been to visit a neighbor and her infant girl. She described how the baby cooed, how rosy her cheeks were, even how she smelled.

Finally Hannah broke into the conversation. "I have a job."

Everyone stopped eating and stared at her.

"With Jacob. I have a job with Jacob." She felt the blush creep up her neck. "I'm going to be helping him with his accounting. It might not be permanent."

"That's *gut*," her father said, reaching for another helping of dumplings. "You always excelled with numbers."

Her mother nodded in agreement. "And you have a real knack for organizing things. Since you've been here you've straightened up every closet and cabinet, even my spices."

"They were a mess."

"Well, now they're in alphabetical order."

"Which makes them easier to find."

"I think it's *wunderbaar*, dear."

It was Matthew who was the most excited about her news. He'd begun tapping his spoon against his plate. "So I will get to see him. You told me that I might not see him anymore, that he'd be helping other kids. But if you're working for him, I'll get to see him. Right? He even said he'd teach me to whistle."

And that was when Hannah knew she'd made

a big mistake. Possibly she'd found a way to help her parents, but in the process she had delayed the inevitable. She could tell by the sparkle in her son's eyes that he didn't realize Jacob was not a part of their family, not even really their friend except in the most broad sense of the word.

The elation she'd felt at landing the job slipped away. She would need to be very careful, not with her own emotions—which weren't an issue at all since she was not attracted to Jacob Schrock—but with Matthew's.

She would protect her son.

Whether from financial hardship that might push him out of his home or emotional attachments that couldn't possibly last.

## Chapter Five

Jacob spent Saturday catching up on projects that he'd let slide in order to complete Matthew's boardwalk. There was a dresser that he'd promised to redo for Evelyn Yutzy. Her granddaughter had recently arrived in town, moved from Maine back to Indiana, and they'd converted the back porch into a bedroom. It was insulated, so the girl wouldn't freeze, but she needed somewhere to put her clothes.

He had only half-finished the crib for Grace Miller, and her baby was due in two weeks. He couldn't put it off any longer. Then there was the workbench that he'd agreed to make for Paul Fisher. It was good that business was... well, busy. But Jacob's heart was with the playhouses, something that he charged as little as possible for. In order to make a living he had to

take care of the individual work orders as well
as the business projects that he had lined up.

Speaking of which, he was supposed to begin
a cabinetry project on a new house the following
week. He'd written the details down somewhere,
but where? He wasted the next hour looking for
the small sheet of paper, which he eventually
found in his lunch pail.

Normally once he started a project he had no
problem focusing on it, but he found himself lag-
ging further and further behind as the day pro-
gressed. He stopped for lunch and went into his
house, but even there he couldn't help looking
around him and seeing the place through Hannah's eyes. It was pitiful really, and he didn't
know how it had happened.

Dishes were stacked in the sink, where he usually ate standing and staring out the window.
Copies of the *Budget* covered every surface in
the sitting room, along with woodworking magazines that the library gave him when they were
too far out-of-date to display. That seemed ridiculous to Jacob—woodworking wasn't something
that changed from one season to the next. Still,
he enjoyed receiving the old copies and looking
through the magazines. He occasionally found
new ideas to try.

When his childhood home had burned down,
he'd purchased a prefab house and had it deliv-

ered to the property. The building was small, around six hundred square feet, but more than what he needed. The workshop had been left intact. As for the fields, his brother Micah farmed them in addition to his own, which was adjacent to the old homestead.

The workshop was larger than his home. The vast majority of it was filled with supplies, workbenches and projects in various stages of completion. The office was a cornered-off ten-by-ten space. On one side of the room, windows looked out over the fields. On the other, windows allowed him to see into the workshop. As far as mess, it was in worse shape than the house. Jacob's heart was in the projects, not the filing systems, or lack thereof, and that showed. He was attempting to move around stacks of paperwork in the office when his brother Micah tapped on the open door.

"Am I interrupting?"

"*Ya.* Can't you see? I'm making progress on my backed-up carpentry orders."

"Huh. Looks to me like you're tossing papers from one shelf to another." Micah crossed the room, stopped in front of one of the plastic bins and raised the lid. "What is all this stuff?"

"Receipts, I guess."

"What's your system?" Micah pulled out a Subway sandwich receipt, stared at it and then turned it over and stared at the writing on the back.

Jacob snatched it out of his hand and tossed it back into the bin. "If it was something that I felt like I needed to keep, I threw it in a bin. The next year I'd buy another from the discount store and begin tossing things in it. There's one for the past...six years."

Micah let out a long whistle. "No wonder the IRS is interested in you, *bruder*. They must have heard about your filing system."

"The last thing I want to talk about is the IRS."

"*Gut*. Because it's not why I came by."

Jacob grunted as he picked up a bin from the floor and dropped it on the desk. Deciding it looked worse, looked even more disorganized there, he put it back where it was.

"Why did you come by?"

"To invite you to dinner, and don't tell me you have plans."

"I do have plans. I should be out there working." He shifted his gaze and stared through the window into the workshop. He could just make out the corner of Grace Miller's crib. It would probably take him another two hours to finish it.

"Then why aren't you?"

"Why aren't I what?"

"Out there working."

"Because Hannah's coming on Monday, and

if she sees this place like it is, she'll probably turn tail and run."

When his brother grinned and dropped into a chair, Jacob realized that the news was already out about his new bookkeeper. No doubt Micah was here to tease him, and the dinner invitation was just a handy excuse.

"Heard young Matthew likes his caboose train."

"*Ya*, he does. Young kids like him, kids who don't lead normal lives, the little things seem to make a big difference."

"And what about Hannah?"

"What about her?"

"Still as pretty as when she was in school?"

"Seriously? That's what we're going to talk about?"

"Why not? It's the first woman you've shown interest in since your accident."

"I'm not interested in her." Jacob reached up and scratched at his scar. "I'm hiring her to bring some order to this chaos."

"So you don't find her attractive?"

"I didn't say that."

"You do find her attractive, then."

"This is the problem with you."

"Problem with me?"

His brother smiled as if he'd just told the funniest joke. It made Jacob want to chuck the bin of papers he was holding right at his head.

"You always think you know what's best for me, but you don't."

"And you always think that your scars preclude you from dating, but they don't."

"What would you know about scars?"

Micah stood, raised his hands, palms out, and shook his head. "I don't know why we do this every time."

"I know why. You insist on sticking your nose in my business."

"We worry about you. Emily and I both do."

"Would you please stop? Would you just trust me to live my own life the way it's meant to be lived?"

"Alone? Moping over what happened?"

"You weren't there, Micah. Don't pretend that you know what happened. Don't pretend you can understand. I'm the one who pulled their bodies from the fire. I'm the one who didn't get there fast enough."

Micah strode to the door, but he stopped dead in his tracks, the afternoon sunlight that was streaming through the open workshop door spilling over his shoulders. Because his back was to Jacob, his words were muffled, softer, but they hit him just as hard as if they'd been standing face-to-face. "You say that you trust *Gotte*, and yet you won't let anyone into your life. You say that you pray, but you don't believe."

And with that, he trudged back outside, across the field and to his own home—leaving Jacob to wonder why everyone thought they had to fix him. They didn't live in his skin. They didn't look at his scars every morning, and they knew nothing of his guilt and loneliness.

Jacob understood his scars for what they were—the penance that he deserved for not saving his parents from the fire that took their lives.

Hannah had been living back in Goshen long enough that Matthew no longer drew obvious stares when they met for church. She was grateful for that, thankful that their neighbors were learning to accept him.

She looked forward to their church services. Loved the familiar faces she'd grown up seeing and the sound of her bishop's voice—the same man who had baptized her. Other than the loneliness that occasionally plagued her and the constant worry over Matthew's health, she was happy, living again with her family.

Church was held every other Sunday and always at a member's home. This week they were at the Yutzy place, which was on the northwest side of town. A portion of their property bordered the Elkhart River. It was a beautiful, peaceful spot, and Hannah could feel its calming power even as she made her way into the barn where they would have church. The large main room had been cleaned out, the doors and windows flung open, and benches arranged on two sides of a makeshift aisle.

At the back of the benches a few tables had been set up with cups of water and plates of cookies for the youngest children. It was sometimes difficult for them to make it all the way through a three- to four-hour meeting without a small snack.

The service was exactly what she needed to quiet her soul. She'd spent too much time since Friday worrying about the job at Jacob's. She knew she could do the work, but would Matthew be okay without her? Was she doing the right thing? Could the small amount of money she was making help her parents' financial situation?

The questions had spun round and round in her head, but that all stopped when they stood to sing the *Loblied*. The words of the hymn reminded her of the good things in her life, the things that *Gotte* had given her. She forgot for a moment the tragedy of losing her husband and the trials of having a special needs son.

Once the service was over and she'd finished helping in the serving line, she went to find her sisters. Both Beth and Sharon were in the last trimester of their pregnancies. In fact, their babies were due only a few weeks apart. They'd tried to help in the serving line and had been shooed away.

"Finally we get you to ourselves," Sharon said. The oldest of the three girls, it had taken her some time to become pregnant after marrying. The twins were two lovely girls full of energy and laughter and a tiny bit of mischief. Another six years had passed before Sharon had finally become pregnant again. She and her husband were hoping for a boy, just to balance things out a bit.

Beth had one daughter, ten-year-old Naomi. She'd had Naomi when she was very young, only seventeen. There had been some problems, and she thought that she couldn't have any more children, but her protruding stomach was testament to the fact that *Gotte* had other plans.

Being around them, watching them rest a hand on their baby bumps or sigh as they tried to push up out of a chair caused an ache deep in Hannah's heart. She'd imagined herself pregnant again, had thought she'd have a house full of children like most Amish women. She had been certain that she would remain married to the same man all of her life. She'd never imagined herself as a young widow.

She searched the crowd of children for her son and finally spied Matthew in his chair, pulled up to a checkerboard that had been placed over a tree stump. One of the older boys who had a foot in a cast was playing with him. As she watched, Matthew glanced occasionally at the children who were playing ball, and it seemed to Hannah that an expression of longing crossed his face.

"Tell us about your new job." Beth was the middle child and the negotiator of the family. It was Beth who had convinced Hannah to move home. Hannah hadn't wanted to be a burden to her parents, but Beth had convinced her that home was where she needed to be and that family could never truly be a burden.

"Tell us about Jacob." Sharon's eyes sparkled. She'd always been one to tease. Perhaps because of her work as a midwife, she believed in enjoying life. She saw moments of great joy every day and the occasional tragedy, as well.

"There's nothing to tell about Jacob, and as far as the job…well, I'm fortunate to find work at all." She described her attempts at finding employment in town. She even mimicked the craft shop owner's voice when she asked if Hannah could bring Matt in occasionally so the tourists could gawk at him.

"Maybe she meant well," Beth said.

Sharon rolled her eyes. "And maybe she has no filter, no sense of what is proper and what is improper. Some business owners—and I've seen it in Amish as well as *Englisch*—they become too enamored with how much money they can make. They forget their employees are people."

"Anyway. I suppose I was upset because of the interview, and I had no other ideas of where to apply." Hannah glanced around to be sure no one else was within earshot. Fortunately most of the women had moved to a circle of chairs under the trees, and the men were congregated on the porch or near the ball field. "I confronted Jacob. I walked right up to him and asked him why he hadn't offered me the job."

"Oh my." Beth placed both hands on her belly. "How did he take it?"

"He was surprised, of course. Amish women are supposed to be quiet and meek."

Both Beth and Sharon laughed at that. Sometimes the reputation that Amish women had earned was frustrating, other times it was simply ludicrous. While they did believe that the man was the spiritual head of the house, the women Hannah knew had no trouble voicing their opinion or standing up for themselves.

"What happened then?" Sharon asked.

"He agreed. It's a temporary position until his audit is over. Then we'll see if there's enough work for me to continue."

"Oh, I'm sure there's enough work. He's probably just afraid you wouldn't want a permanent position. I still see his sister-in-law Emily because our homes are fairly close together. The dividing line for our districts is between us. Anyway, she tells me that Jacob's a real wonder with the woodworking…"

"Have you seen the playhouse he made?" Beth interrupted. "It's amazing. I stopped by yesterday and even Naomi spent an hour out in it, and she's ten. I haven't seen her in a playhouse since the summer she was six and her *dat* knocked together something from old barn lumber. Wasn't even really a lean-to, but she would drag every little friend that came over out to play there."

"What are you worried about, Hannah?" Sharon studied her sister. "You might as well share with us. Is it Matthew? Is he feeling all right?"

"Matthew's fine, I guess."

"You guess?" Now Beth was on alert. "Tell us. What's happened?"

"Nothing has happened." Hannah blew out a sigh of exasperation. "I'm starting a new job that I know nothing about."

"Which you asked for—" Beth reminded her.

"I'm leaving Matthew with *Mamm*, and she has enough to do."

"I've already spoken to her about that. She's welcome to bring Matthew by anytime—"

"You're seven months pregnant, Sharon, and you're still delivering babies. The last thing you need is—"

"My nephew? Actually I do need to spend time with him and so do my girls. He's family, Hannah. We want him around."

"Naomi asks me every day if Matthew can come over." Beth rubbed the side of her stomach. "We'll help *Mamm*. Don't worry about that."

Which effectively shut down her doubts about leaving Matthew during the day.

"I'm not sure it will be enough money," she admitted. "The amount they owe? I was surprised. I knew they'd helped me and Matt, but I didn't know… I didn't know they'd sacrificed so much."

"It's what families do, Hannah." Sharon took on her older sister tone. "You've forgotten because you moved away. You and David moved, what was it…"

"Three months. We moved three months after we were wed."

"Right, and I understand how you'd want to try the community in Wisconsin, but while you were there maybe you learned to be independent, maybe too independent."

"Now you're with family, and we take care of one another," Beth chimed in.

Hannah didn't need a lecture about family. Yes, she appreciated her parents and sisters and brothers-in-law, but they didn't understand just how much of a burden Matthew's disability could be. They hadn't experienced an emergency run to the hospital because of a minor cold that had quickly morphed into pneumonia.

"Back to the money…" she said.

"Simon has some saved, which he has offered to *Dat*." Sharon's husband worked at the RV factory in Shipshewana two days a week. The rest of the time he farmed their land.

"Carl does too." Beth raised her foot and stared at her swollen ankle. "*Dat* told me he doesn't want to take it unless he's sure it will cover the balance. He doesn't want to drain our savings for a place he might lose anyway."

And there it was—the real fear of losing their childhood home. It was common for Amish to up and move for a variety of reasons—a disagreement with the way the church district was being run, a rumor that land was more plentiful and less expensive in another state, even a vague restlessness to see somewhere different.

But this wasn't that.

This was being forced from your home, and to Hannah that made it a much graver thing.

"How much will you make?" Sharon asked.

Hannah told them the hourly wage she'd asked for and how many hours she thought she could work. "Not a full forty," she explained. "I told him that I still want to take Matthew to his appointments."

"We could do that for you."

"I know you could, Sharon. I know you both would, and *danki* for offering." She smoothed her apron out over her lap, then ran her hand across it again before looking up to meet her sisters' gazes. "This is something I'd like to continue to do, if I can."

Both sisters nodded as if they understood, and maybe they did.

Sharon scrounged around in her purse for a receipt and a pen. On the back of the receipt she added up what Simon had saved, what Carl had pulled together and what Hannah would make in the next month minus any taxes she would have to pay.

"You saw the letter." Sharon chewed on the end of the pen. "How much did it say they owed?"

When Hannah quoted the amount, Beth leaned closer to the paper. "We're a little short."

"But we still have thirty days."

"Twenty-eight." Hannah glanced over at her mother, who was sitting with the other women and watching the *youngies* play ball. "Twenty-eight days. Between now and then, we need to find a way to come up with the difference."

## Chapter Six

Hannah tried on all three of her dresses Monday morning. The gray one made her look like a grandmother. The green was a bit snug. Had she actually gained weight since moving home? She could thank her mother's cooking for that. The dark blue was her oldest, but it was all that was left other than what she wore to Sunday services, and she wouldn't dare wear that to Jacob's workshop.

Frustrated that she cared about how she looked, she donned the dark blue dress, a fresh apron and her *kapp*. One last shrug at her reflection in the window, and she walked down the hall to Matthew's room. She didn't enter, though. Instead she paused at the door. She heard her son moving around, and yet he hadn't called out to her. That was a good sign. It meant he'd slept well.

She turned the knob and walked into the room.

The sky had barely begun to lighten outside, but she pulled up the shades and then sat on his bed. He smiled up at her, curling over on his side.

"You look *gut*—pretty."

*"Danki."*

"Are you excited?"

"About my job?"

*"Ya."* He reached out for her apron strings, ran them through his fingers. "I would be excited, if I was going to spend all day with Jacob. Why can't I go? Please…"

He drew out the last word, and Hannah almost laughed. It sounded so normal, so everyday, that she actually didn't mind the whining.

"We've been over this. I will be working with numbers all day—"

"I can write my numbers."

"Yes, but I'm afraid it's a bit more complicated than that."

"And Jacob will be working."

"He will."

"On a playhouse?"

"I don't know."

Matthew considered that for a moment, and then he said what must have been on his mind all along. "I'd like to see some of his playhouses. They're not all trains—I know that because he described a few. I'd like to see what the others look like."

"Would you now?"

"Do you think that maybe…maybe we could?"

Hannah hesitated. She didn't want to encourage this infatuation that her son had for her boss. At the same time, as Sally had pointed out, it was natural for Matthew to look up to men in their community. "If they're in the area, and he tells me where they are…well, I don't see why we couldn't drive by when we're out on errands."

Matthew's smile was all the answer she needed. How could such a small thing bring him such joy? How was it that he managed to accept his condition so easily without bitterness? He pushed himself into an upright position and raised his arms for Hannah's father to pick him up.

"I didn't hear you come in," Hannah said.

"Because I'm as quiet as a cat and as quick as a panther." Her father winked at her as he carried Matthew out of the room.

"Have you ever seen a panther, *Daddi*?"

Matthew had slept well, woke up with no signs of a cold or infection and was showing a real interest in the things going on around him. It was a good day for certain, so why was a part of Hannah still worried?

She walked back into the room to fetch Matthew's clothes for the day.

"He'll be fine." Her father paused to kiss the top of her head, which made her feel like a small child again. It also made her feel loved and cared for. "And I appreciate your taking the job. I hope you know you don't have to."

"I know, *Dat*, but I want to help."

"Your *mamm* and I appreciate that."

"It's important—to be able to stay in this place, to raise Matthew surrounded by familiar things and people."

"Familiar to you, but not so much to Matt." Her father glanced across the hall into the bathroom to be sure that Matthew was fine without him. With a nod to indicate that the boy was all right, he sat down beside her on the bed. "You know, Hannah, it could be that *Gotte* has other plans for us, that we're not meant to stay in this house or even in this community."

"But you would want to…if you could. Right?"

"Things turn out best for the people who make the best of the way things turns out."

"Really, *Dat*? Your answer is a proverb?"

His smile eased the anxiousness in her heart and reminded her of Matthew. The two were more alike than she had realized.

"If you enjoy the job and if you can help Jacob, then you have my blessing. Listen to me closely though, Hannah. If you find it's too much pressure, I want you to remember that your priority is your son, not how much money you can make."

"*Ya, Dat*, but it's something I want to do."

He nodded as if he understood, and maybe he did.

Hannah barely ate any breakfast, though she did help to clean up the kitchen. After going over the morning instructions one last time with her mother, the entire family shooed her out of the house.

She hurried toward Dolly, who her father had already hitched to the buggy, turning back to call out, "I left Jacob's phone number on the sheet."

"We have it, but we won't need it."

"And I'm sorry I can't go to the store for you."

"Stop worrying. Matt and I will take care of it."

"I'll try. See you around four thirty."

Her mother had actually packed her a lunch. She should have done that herself.

Clucking to Dolly, she set off down the road.

When was the last time that she'd gone somewhere without her son? When was the last time she'd been alone? She found herself enjoying the drive, smiling at the other drivers on the road—both Amish and *Englisch*—and noting how well the flower gardens had bloomed. Every home she passed had some spot of color brightening their lawn, or bordering their vegetable rows or in pots on the front porch. Goshen was a tourist destination, nearly as popular as Shipshewana, and the houses and businesses made every effort to present a clean, colorful picture.

It took her less than twenty minutes to reach Jacob's place, and she was embarrassed to find herself there a full thirty minutes early.

"He'll think I'm overeager." She shook her head as she pulled down the lane. So what if she was? What did it matter? She was impatient to finally be of some help instead of a burden, and if she were honest, a little bit of her was looking forward to the quiet and challenge of a column of numbers.

Jacob was sitting on the front porch of the workshop when Hannah pulled down the lane. He shouldn't have been surprised that she was early. She seemed like the kind of person that would be.

By the time she set the brake on the buggy, he was standing there beside her. He took the reins and slipped them around the waist-high tie bar situated a few feet from the front of the shop.

"I can't believe that I've never been here."

She seemed a bit out of breath and flushed and

beautiful. He shook the thought out of his mind and tried to pay attention to what she was saying.

"Not even when we were kids?"

"Maybe for church. I can't remember."

"The place looked different then."

He pointed to the area where his parents' home had been. "Micah and I cleared off the site after the fire and extended my mother's garden to cover the old homestead. We thought it would be a nice way to remember them."

"It's lovely, and I'm so very sorry about your parents."

"Every life is complete." He said the words without thinking about them. It was what they believed, what they always said during such times. It was only during those terrible nights when he relived the destruction of the fire in his nightmares that he struggled with the concept. In the light of day, with Hannah smiling at him, it was easy enough to believe that *Gotte* had a plan and purpose for each of their lives and that sometimes that plan was beyond their understanding.

"And you live over there?"

He glanced back at the twenty-foot prefab. It looked rather pitiful and shabby in the morning light. He'd done nothing to spruce it up—no porch or rocking chairs or flowers. It wasn't really a home, and he knew that. "*Ya.* It's temporary."

"How long have you lived there?"

"Six years."

Hannah looked directly at him for the first time since arriving, a look of surprise coloring her features. When he started laughing, she did too. He didn't mind her seeing the humor in the situation, mainly because she was laughing with him instead of at him.

Finally Hannah said, "I suppose it's enough for a bachelor."

"It is. Let me show you the workshop."

He took her through the main room, explaining the various stages that each project went through from commission to design, cutting, assembling, sanding and finishing.

"There's a lot to it," Hannah said.

*"Ya."* He was proud of his workshop. Every tool had a place. He cleaned each item after he used it and placed it on a peg on the wall. Sawdust was swept up each evening. Small projects were kept in large cubbies under one window that ran almost the entire length of the room. Bigger projects were lined up along the other wall. Design plans for playhouses were rolled and stored in smaller bins behind his worktable. A potbelly stove, rocking chair, hand-hooked rug made by his sister-in-law and small refrigerator adorned one corner.

The room looked better than where he lived.

"Bathroom's back in that corner."

"Place smells nice—like a lumberyard."

"The office is over here." He pointed to the room in the opposite corner.

Hannah raised an eyebrow and motioned for him to lead the way.

When they walked into the room, Jacob experienced a flash of panic. Who would want to work in this cramped little space all day? He'd made a feeble attempt to clean it up, but there was no hiding the fact that it had been neglected for years.

"This was my father's office. As you can see, I haven't used it much." He walked to the shelves and glanced at the items that had been there since the day his father had died. He hadn't wanted to move a thing, hadn't felt like he should. Fortunately, Hannah wouldn't need shelves, as there was a large desk.

Hannah stood there, frozen, letting her gaze drift from left to right and then back again. He waited for her to say something, but for once she seemed speechless.

"These tubs are full of receipts, and as you can see, each is labeled with the year."

*"Ya?"*

"I also put in the deposit slips each year, so you should be able to figure out what I earned versus what I spent. I tried to keep up with what people paid me by noting it on slips of paper, and you'll find a few of those."

"Slips of paper…"

"I'm afraid that after I figured my taxes each year, I probably tossed the worksheets, though I did keep a copy of the returns and they're in the box, as well."

Hannah raised the lid off one of the tubs, stared inside for a moment and then quickly closed the lid. "Well. I see I have my work cut out for me."

"I cleared off the desk."

*"Danki."*

"And there's a ledger, which I've never used."

"Obviously."

Jacob wondered if she would tell him that it was too big a job, that he was crazy to have been so lax with his record keeping, that he deserved whatever penalties the IRS threw at him. Instead she set her purse and lunch bag on the desk.

"You can write down your hours on that pad, and I'll pay you on Monday for the previous week's work if that's okay."

"That will be fine." Hannah touched the desk chair, which looked as if it might fall over.

How long had he had that thing? His dad had purchased it in some garage sale years and years ago.

"I'll go and look after Dolly."

"Oh, I can do that. I just wanted to make sure you hadn't changed your mind first."

He gave her an odd look, shook his head and said, "I'll be back in a minute."

And then he turned and left, because if he stood looking at Hannah King one more minute, wearing her pretty blue dress with the morning light shining through on her freshly laundered *kapp* and lightly freckled face…he'd start daydreaming again, and that was the very last thing that he needed to do.

Once Jacob left the office, Hannah glanced over at the bins in horror.

She stepped closer to the window and stared out at the fall day, watching as Jacob moved Dolly into the shade and fetched her a bucket of water. A man who cared properly for animals was a good man. Why hadn't Jacob ever married? Why did he live in a tiny trailer on this large piece of land? Surely he could afford better.

At least it looked as if business was booming.

She was good at math, and she had helped her husband with his business records in Wisconsin, but she'd never seen a mess like this before.

She stepped closer to one of the bins, opened the lid and peered inside. She pawed through the stack of paper—all sizes of paper, from a receipt from a cash register, to a bill that looked as if it had been scribbled on across the back, to a Publishers Clearing House flyer.

Looking closer, she sent up a silent thanks that at least she could read his handwriting.

Jacob walked back into the room, and she slammed the lid shut again.

"Problem?"

"Why would you say that?"

"I don't know. You look as if you've seen a runaway buggy."

She tried to smile. "Nope. No buggies. Just lots of receipts."

Jacob's smile vanished. "I know it's a lot of work, Hannah, but at least I kept the receipts separated by year."

"*Ya*, I see that."

"Six years. Six bins. That helps. Right?"

"I'm sure it will."

He stepped closer and reached out to put his hand on her arm.

"Hannah, I need to tell you something."

She didn't move, didn't breathe.

"I appreciate what you're doing, more than you could know."

She tried to listen to his words, but her heart had taken off at a galloping pulse, and she was staring at his hand on her arm. His fingers against her skin stirred something inside of Hannah, something she didn't realize she still possessed. Mixed with hope, and sprinkled with a dash of optimism—all things she hadn't felt in quite some time.

Jacob seemed to notice her discomfort. He dropped his hand to his side, then fiddled with the sleeve he'd rolled up to his elbows. "You're a real godsend."

"I haven't done anything yet." She laughed nervously and moved around the desk, running her fingers across the wood.

"I guess I'm headed out for the day. Just… make a list of any questions, and we'll go over them this afternoon or first thing tomorrow morning."

"Jacob—"

He seemed to brace himself against what she was about to say.

"I should thank you—for the job."

"Thank me?"

"The way I asked, *nein*, demanded, you to give it to me—that wasn't proper."

"You were right, though."

"I was?"

"This place is a mess. Even I can see it."

"There's a lot here for one person to take care of. You probably should have hired help earlier. I hope I can rise to the challenge."

"I remember how you were with numbers in school."

"That was a long time ago."

He'd stuck his thumbs under his suspenders and walked to the door, but now he turned back toward her. "I did know about your father's difficulties. I just wasn't sure you'd want to leave Matthew."

"And I don't, but my parents and my sisters... everyone is going to pitch in and help. That's what family does, *ya*?"

Instead of answering, Jacob fetched his hat from a hook on the wall and rammed it on his head. "If anyone calls, please write down a message."

"Oh, you're leaving?"

"*Ya.* I just said I was headed out."

"I thought you meant...to the fields or something."

"My *bruder* works the fields on this place. I work here in the workshop or out on jobs."

"So that's where you're going? To a job?"

"One of the local builders has me putting in cabinets this week, in the new homes on the north side of town."

"Oh..."

"Some weeks I work here in the workshop."

"I see."

"I prefer to work on the playhouses whenever it's possible, but the cabinetry work—"

"It pays the bills."

"*Ya*. That it does." He looked out the office window.

Hannah wondered if he was stalling, though she couldn't imagine why. He seemed quite uncomfortable with her there and no doubt couldn't wait to be gone.

"I'll just get to work on these receipts, then. Most current year first?"

"I suppose."

"Okay…"

"I guess I'll see you this afternoon."

Hannah pushed her *kapp* strings back. "I planned to leave around four thirty."

"Weren't you taking Matthew to therapy today?"

"*Nein*, that's tomorrow and, well… I thought we'd wait and see how much work there actually is for me to do, and whether it's going to be a problem getting everything in order before your audit."

She wanted to say something more, to somehow put him at ease, but she had no idea how. Then she remembered the reason she was there.

"The IRS letter, you still have it?"

"Oh, *ya*. It's in the top right drawer. I guess you need to look it over."

"And you're sure you wouldn't rather take this all to an accountant?"

"I did go and see one, but the price they quoted was quite high."

"I'll try, Jacob."

"Which is all I can ask. The letter seems pretty straightforward as far as what they want to see, which is why I need you."

"They don't take boxes full of receipts?"

"Apparently not." He pulled his hat off, turned it round and round in his hands. "If there are any other supplies you need, there's petty cash in the bottom drawer."

Jacob left so abruptly that Hannah stood staring after him for a moment. She'd spent much of the night worrying about how she'd be able to work with him in such close proximity. Apparently that wouldn't be a problem. He wouldn't even be on the property. Hannah waited until she saw his buggy drive past the workshop and down the lane before returning inside to the small office.

Though he'd apparently made an effort to clean the mess off the top of the desk, dust lay thick across its surface.

A clean desktop is the sign of a cluttered desk drawer. The proverb popped into her mind unbidden. Walking around to the other side of the

desk, she spied what she'd known was somewhere close by...a box stuffed with everything
that had been on top of it.

The window was smeared with dirt, and the
floor hadn't been swept in ages.

He wasn't paying her to clean the office. On
the other hand, who could work in these con-
ditions? Would the IRS agent want to receive
books covered in dust and grime? Not to mention what this room would do to her clean apron.

She tsked as she walked back through the
main room in search of cleaning supplies. Finally she found them in a corner on the far side
of the building—a broom, mop bucket, rags and
even furniture polish. She carted it all back to
the office and set to work.

Two hours later the place was sparkling.
Opening the window had allowed a fresh, clean
breeze to blow through. The desk was made
from a beautiful dark cherry wood, and it shone
from the furniture polish she'd used. She ran her
palm across the surface and wondered if Jacob
had built it. The chair was a real hazard, so she
walked back into the main room and found a
stool that was at least sturdy.

The box beside the desk held a tape dispenser,
some pens, a stapler and rubber bands that had
long ago aged to the point that they snapped
when she tried to put one around a bundle of re-

ceipts. She dug through the supplies and found a box of pencils (though there was no sharpener that she could see), and a pad of paper.

As she ate her lunch, she began making a list of supplies, then found the petty cash box and placed both next to her purse. She'd stop by the general store while Matthew was at therapy the next day.

Finally she pulled the most recent bin over to the desk.

An hour later she had a list of questions for Jacob.

She couldn't begin entering things in the ledger until she spoke with him, and apparently that wouldn't be until the next morning. She could tape up receipts, but even the tape was yellowed and old, which left her quite a few hours to kill before she had to leave. Glancing around the small office, she decided one thing she could do was clear a bigger workspace.

She walked into the main room of the workshop and snooped around until she found two empty boxes. Taking them back into the office, she cleared off the items on the shelves. Dusty canning jars filled with an odd variety of nails and screws and even buttons. A broken pipe. A spool of thread. Some very old *Farmers' Almanac* editions dating back forty years.

She couldn't fathom why he was keeping most

of the items, and she was tempted to scrape all of it into the trash bin. The basket by her desk wasn't large enough. Plus, it wasn't her place to decide what was and wasn't trash.

It was her place to put his financial records in order, and to do that she needed more space.

It took a little pushing and grunting, but she'd managed to move the desk closer to the shelves.

Now she'd be able to easily move between both, and she could also look out the window instead of having it at her back. She poured another mug of coffee from her thermos, snagged a cookie from the lunch her mother had packed and moved to the front porch. Sitting there she looked out over Jacob's land.

It was *gut* land. She could tell that, though she was only a farmer's daughter, not a farmer herself. It looked well cared for, so Jacob's brother must spend a fair amount of time working there. But the place that Jacob lived? She stared at it a minute before shaking her head in disbelief and going back into the office. There was no understanding the ways of men, especially confirmed bachelors.

Having no way to put off the inevitable, she once again pulled over the most recent bin containing the previous year's receipts and began pulling out scraps of paper. Perhaps she could stack them together by what appeared to be type—supplies, income notations, even hours spent on a job that were scribbled on a flyer about their annual school auction.

The rest of the afternoon flew by and the list of questions grew and grew until they filled up two sheets of paper. She was surprised to look up and see the hands on the clock had passed four. She was thinking of gathering her things to leave when she heard the clatter of a buggy. She wasn't too surprised when she glanced out the window and saw it was Jacob. Perhaps he had finished his day's work early.

She was standing in the doorway looking around in satisfaction when he walked up behind her.

Jacob had been a little afraid he'd arrive home to find that Hannah had left. The last girl had put a note on the desk and told him he didn't owe her for the morning's work. She'd also suggested he hire an accountant. It seemed that Hannah was made of tougher stuff. Perhaps if she'd survived the first day, it meant that she'd see the project through to the end. It wasn't so much that he wanted her around, but he was a man who could admit that he needed help. As far as accounting and the IRS went, Jacob needed all the help he could possibly find.

He walked up behind Hannah. Her tiny frame

blocked the doorway, but he could see over her head into the office. Something looked different, but he couldn't put his finger on what it was.

"Did you have a *gut* day?"

*"Ya."* She smiled back at him and stepped aside so he could see. "I think I accomplished a lot."

He stared at the office, or at least he thought it was his office, but it looked nothing like the room he'd left earlier that morning. He reached out for the door frame to keep from stumbling backward.

"What did you do?"

"What did I do?"

"What…" He walked into the office, strode across to the shelves that had held the precious mementos from his father. "Where did you put my father's things?"

"Do you mean the broken pipe and the jar full of mismatched doodads?"

Jacob bit back the first retort that came to mind. He closed his eyes—determined to count to ten—and made it to three. *"Ya*, those things. Where are they?"

"I didn't throw them away, Jacob. I put them in boxes and stored them in the utility closet."

"Why would you do such a thing?"

"Because I needed more space than the top of that desk."

"I could have built you a workbench."

"But the shelves were right there, and you weren't here to build me a workbench. What was I supposed to do all day?"

"Who moved the desk?"

"I did."

"By yourself?"

"Yes, by myself. It wasn't that hard. I got behind it and—"

"Pushed. You pushed it across the floor."

He squatted, ran his hand over a scratch in the wooden floor.

"Did I do that? I'm… I'm sorry, but this is a barn. Am I right? It's not like it's your living room."

No, his living room was part of a prefab house that held no meaning at all in his life, no memories of his parents. All he had that remained of his childhood was this old barn, the office, the garden that his mother had loved.

He clenched his jaw, determined not to speak harsh words. What was the old proverb? Think before you speak, but don't speak all you think.

Walking to the window, he stared out at his mother's garden. At least Hannah hadn't pulled up any of the plants in her compulsion to reorganize things. Suddenly he noticed how clean the windows were, and the floor, even the walls looked as if they'd been dusted.

"Did you do any of the work you were supposed to do today?"

"Excuse me?"

"I'm not paying you to clean windows or dust shelves."

"As I think I explained, I need those shelves, and I also need more light in this room if I'm to stare at your receipts all day."

"So you did at least look at them."

"Which was all I could do since I have no idea what your scribbling means."

"My scribbling?"

"When you actually took the time to label what you'd written onto some scrap of paper."

Hannah stomped toward the desk and yanked the bottom drawer open.

"You cleaned out the drawers too?"

For her answer she pulled out her purse and slammed the drawer shut. "I'll be going now."

"Going?"

"And if you expect me to work in this small, stuffy, poorly lit office, then I suggest you get used to the changes."

"Oh, is that so?"

"And don't bother offering to hitch up Dolly. I'm quite capable of doing it myself."

# Chapter Seven

Hannah was so angry her ears felt hot.

No doubt they had been bright red as she stormed out of the office. What did she care if Jacob Schrock knew how aggravated she was?

Hitching up Dolly helped to burn up some of her anger. By the time she'd pulled out onto the two-lane road, she was composing her resignation letter in her head.

But as she drove the short distance to her parents' farm, she realized that she couldn't quit, not yet. She needed a job, and she was good at accounting. She could even bring order out of Jacob's chaos, if he'd let her.

Glancing out at the countryside, it struck her what day it was—the anniversary of the accident. Had her emotions recognized that all along? Was that why she was so emotional?

It wasn't until she was pulling into the lane,

arching her neck forward to look for Matthew, that she realized the other source of her anxiety. It was true that Jacob's office had been a mess, and she had needed a better workspace, but it was also true that she was nervous about being away from Matthew all day. She was his mother. She should be there.

Her father met her at the door to the barn. "I'll take care of Dolly. How was your first day?"

"Fine," she lied. "Matthew?"

"In his playhouse. He's had a *gut* day."

Those words eased the worry that threatened to choke the breath out of her.

Had she become a helicopter parent? She knew practically nothing about helicopters. She'd seen one a few times, but she'd never ridden in one. She didn't know how that term could relate to her parenting abilities, but she'd seen the article in a magazine's headlines. Helicopter Parents' Horrendous Kids.

She'd actually paged through it as she waited for the woman in front of her to check out at the supermarket.

According to the article there were ten ways that she'd managed to mess up Matthew's life, and he wasn't even five years old. Among other things, she needed to start letting him work out his social issues, involve herself less in his day-to-day life and in general stop fussing over him.

She'd shaken her head in mock despair and placed the magazine back on the rack.

But it wasn't mock despair she was feeling now.

Maybe she really had messed up his life.

She'd been gone less than eight hours, but it felt like she hadn't seen him in a week. The truth was that she couldn't stand to have him out of her sight.

He might need her.

And she was afraid to let him fail.

Hadn't he had enough disappointment in life?

She envisioned outlandish things happening to him.

Just that morning she'd worried that he might fall out of the buggy if her mother didn't make sure the door was shut. Her mother had been driving a buggy longer than Hannah had been alive.

Was it so wrong to worry though? Matthew was disabled. He was special, and he had special needs.

She pulled in a deep breath, put the parenting article out of her mind and headed for the train.

The next thirty minutes she spent listening to Matthew tell her about his day, as he pretended they were passengers headed to Alaska, and trying not to laugh as he wheeled himself back and forth across the train with the conductor hat on his head.

Her mood had improved dramatically by the time they went inside to help with dinner.

After they'd eaten and were clearing the dishes from the table, her temper had cooled enough that she'd begun to feel ashamed of herself. Her father had taken Matthew to the barn to help settle the horses for the evening. She peeked out the window, didn't see them and refocused on the plate she was drying.

"Problem, dear?"

"Why do you say that?"

"Because you just put a clean plate in the oven."

"I did?"

"Why don't you sit at the table and start shelling the purple hull peas? You can tell me about your day."

So she did. She told her mother about being overwhelmed by the task of preparing Jacob's files for a tax audit, of cleaning up his office with complete disregard to his preferences and of worrying Matthew might fall out of the buggy.

To her surprise, her mother started laughing and then couldn't stop.

"I don't see what's so funny."

Pulling off her reader glasses, her mother swiped at her eyes.

"I can't even tell if you're laughing or crying."

"I'm laughing."

"But why?"

Instead of answering, her mother put the kettle on to boil and dropped two bags of decaf raspberry tea into two mugs. She set a plate of oatmeal cookies between them and smiled at Hannah.

"You've always been an organizer."

"I have?"

"One day when you were little, I found you sorting through your father's socks, lining them up from most stained to least stained."

"I don't remember that."

The kettle on the stove whistled, and soon Hannah found herself holding a steaming cup of raspberry tea. She inhaled deeply and smiled over the rim at her mother.

"I remember organizing your button jar. It was one of my favorite things to do."

"One time I found them by color."

"And one time by size."

The memory touched a tender spot in Hannah's heart. It reminded her of a time before life had become so complicated. She reached for an oatmeal cookie. It was sweet, crunchy around the edges and full of raisins. It was bliss after a long, trying day.

"I suppose I might have been a bit hasty in scooping everything into the box."

"Perhaps those items had some sentimental meaning to Jacob."

"I don't see how."

"What were they?"

"An old pipe, some glass jars, old copies of *Farmers' Almanac*…"

"Sounds like things that could have belonged to his father."

"But there was nothing valuable there."

"The office used to be his father's?"

"I suppose. That would also explain why he was upset that I moved the desk."

"You moved it?"

Hannah waved away her concern. "Wasn't so heavy when I pushed. I needed to move it to have better light, but perhaps I should have asked first."

"Perhaps…" Her mother reached for a cookie, chewed it thoughtfully and finally said, "You and Jacob are alike."

"No, we're not."

"Hear me out."

Hannah rolled her eyes and immediately felt twelve instead of twenty-six.

"You've both been dealt quite a blow."

"I suppose."

"You've both learned to live with that, and to

keep going regardless of the strange and terrible turns that life can take."

Hannah shrugged.

"And you've both kept yourself apart from others."

"We're supposed to do that. We're Amish." She drew out the last word, as if her mother were hard of hearing.

"*Ya*, I'm aware, but you know very well that's not what I mean."

Hannah motioned for her to go on. Somehow it was easier to accept her mother's advice, her insights, when she was eating one of her favorite desserts.

"Neither of you are used to dealing with other people on a regular basis."

"We both have family."

"True."

"We go to the store."

"*Ya.*"

"See people at church."

"You know what I mean, Hannah King, so don't act like you don't."

Hannah popped the remainder of the second cookie in her mouth. She'd regret eating all of it later, but for now it made her feel marginally better.

"You're saying that because we don't date.

Well, I don't. As far as I know, Jacob takes a different girl out in his buggy every night."

"Doubtful."

"I suppose."

"I'm only saying that you're both used to doing things your own way and not asking others their opinion."

"So I've lost my social skills?"

"Pretty much."

"Great."

"But the good news is you have another chance to improve those skills tomorrow."

Hannah groaned and pushed herself up from the table. "Any suggestions for how I should do that?"

"You could start with an apology."

Apologizing was the last thing that she wanted to do. She patted her mother on the shoulder and went in search of her son. After she'd helped Matthew with his bath, tucked him in, read a bedtime story and listened to his prayers, she knew what she needed to do. So she went to her room, spent a few minutes in prayer and finally opened her well-worn Bible. It didn't take long to find the verse that was weighing on her heart. She thumbed through the pages until she found the book of Matthew, the fifth chapter, beginning in the twenty-third verse.

*Therefore if thou bring thy gift to the altar,*

*and there rememberest that thy brother hath ought against thee; leave thy gift before the altar, and go thy way; first be reconciled to thy brother, and then come and offer thy gift.*

There didn't seem to be much wiggle room in Christ's words. Obviously she had offended Jacob. After speaking with her mother, she understood that clearly. Now all she had to do was work up the courage to admit that she'd been wrong, she'd acted hastily, and she was sorry to have raised her voice and left so abruptly. It shouldn't be that hard of a thing to get through, and even if it was, she was pretty sure apologizing would be the first item on her list at work the next day.

Relief washed over Jacob when he heard Hannah's buggy approaching. He'd convinced himself that he'd blown it and that she wasn't coming back.

He pretended to be busy working on a coffee table when she walked inside.

"I thought you'd be at your job site already."

"I thought you might not come."

Their eyes locked for what seemed like a lifetime, and finally Hannah smiled ruefully, walked toward him and sat down across from his workbench.

"I did consider resigning…"

"You wouldn't be the first."

"But then I realized that I need this job."

"Hannah, we both know you can find a better job—one that pays more and doesn't require you to mop the floor." He glanced up at her and then stared back down at the coffee table. Had he been sanding or staining it?

"Maybe I could find another job, but I didn't like what was out there."

"Apparently you didn't like what was in here, either."

"Jacob, I am sorry for raising my voice at you yesterday and for disregarding your father's things."

Jacob's head snapped up, and he found Hannah staring at him, a look of regret on her face.

"I should have asked first."

He smiled for the first time that day as the knot in his stomach slowly unwound. "*Dat* would have told me to clean the office long ago. He always said he was going to, but then he'd get distracted by something else."

"Still, those items were special to you, and if you want them on the shelves I'll put them back."

"No need to do that."

"I'm not sorry for cleaning or moving the furniture, but if you don't want to pay me for those hours, I understand."

"You're so *gut* at cleaning, maybe you could

tackle my house." When she straightened up in alarm, he said, "I'm kidding. What I mean is that I've probably grown used to things being a bit messy."

Hannah ran a finger across the top of his workbench and held it up. "Your workshop is clean enough. See? No dust."

No dust. That meant he had been staining the piece he was working on, not sanding it, which also explained the rag in his hand. Honestly, what was wrong with his train of thought these days?

"*Ya*, having a clean workspace is important when I'm staining wood, and it helps to keep my tools in good condition." He sighed and grimaced, knowing what he needed to say next. "I'm sure having a clean and functional work area is important for your work too. I'm sorry I overreacted."

"So we're *gut*?"

"We are."

"Great." She hopped off the bench. "Oh, one more thing, though. I would like to leave early on days that Matt has therapy appointments. So today I'll work through lunch and leave at one."

"That isn't a problem."

"You're sure?"

"I thought we had already agreed on that.

You'll be taking off early on therapy days—
Tuesday, Wednesday and Friday. Right?"

"Right. It's possible I could take some of the
work with me and do it in the office waiting
room."

"Only if you want to."

She walked across to the office and then pivoted to face him. "Why aren't you at the job site
today?"

"The builder didn't get all the supplies in on
time, but he was expecting a shipment later
today. I guess I'll head back over tomorrow."

"Okay. Do you have time to answer some
questions?"

"I can try."

"You might want to bring a mug of coffee."

"For myself or both of us?"

Her smile broadened, and Jacob realized she
was one of the prettiest women he knew. The
fact that she had called him on the wreck of an
office he'd wanted her to work in? He could see
now that he'd deserved that.

"Bring a cup for both of us. I have a lot of
questions."

Hannah told herself she needed to get over
her nerves if she was going to work in close
proximity with Jacob every day. She felt like
a schoolgirl with a crush. What was she think-

ing? She did not have romantic feelings for Jacob Schrock. She was a grown woman with a young child and a job. She was way beyond crushes.

Jacob pulled the old office chair back into the office. "Don't look at me that way. It's not for you to sit on. I brought it for myself."

"*Gut.* What I mean is, I was afraid it would collapse under me."

Jacob's grin widened as he handed her a mug of coffee. "Sorry I don't have anything sweet to go with this. I'm not actually a baker."

Hannah popped up, retrieved her quilted lunch bag and pulled out a Tupperware container filled with snickerdoodle squares. "Apparently my *mamm* thinks this job is going to require massive amounts of sugar."

The food and coffee helped to ease what tension remained between them.

Hannah pulled out the notes she'd made the day before and began firing questions at him.

"What does the notation *R* mean?"

"Money I received for a job."

"And *P* means…"

"Something I paid for."

"Okay. I'd sort of figured those out, but what in the world is *Q*?"

"Means I had a question. Wasn't sure if the receipt was important or not."

"Give me an example."

"Buggy repairs."

"Excuse me?"

"*Englischers* take off car repairs…"

"*Nein.* They take off mileage, and they're allowed so much per mile for traveling to and from locations that are job related."

"So can I take off mileage?"

She tapped her pen against the pad of paper and made a notation.

"What did you write down?"

"A note to call your accountant and ask him or her."

"I don't have an accountant. That's why I'm in this mess."

"You're in this mess because you are ignorant…"

Jacob choked on his coffee.

"By that I mean you're uneducated in the ways of *Englisch* laws. There are going to be questions I can't answer, Jacob. We need to ask a professional."

"*Gut* point."

"I'll make a list and you can call whomever you trust."

Jacob pulled the pad toward him and wrote the name of a Goshen accounting firm across the top of the page, then added the name of the person she should contact.

"You call them. I'm making accountant questions officially a part of your job."

"I imagine they'll bill you for the time."

"It'll still be much less than having them tape up receipts." He leaned back in his chair, causing it to let out an alarming groan, and laced his fingers behind his head. "Do you know how to use the phone?"

"*Ya.* I've used one a few times." She tried not to stare at the muscles bulging in his arms. Who would have thought that a woodworker would be in such good shape?

"So no phone lessons are required."

"I'm a little surprised you have one here in the shop."

"The bishop allows it, and truthfully my mother wanted one. She was always worried one of us would injure ourselves with a table saw. The woman had quite an imagination. Anyway, when the bishop started allowing them for businesses, she ordered one."

"So she could call 911?"

"*Ya.*"

"Did she ever have to?"

"Only when my *dat* was bit by a snake. He wanted to drive himself to the hospital, but she had an ambulance on the way before he could hobble to the horse stall."

"Was it poisonous?"

"Probably not. The critter crawled away, and he didn't have a chance to identify it. The doctors treated him all the same, and *Mamm* was forever saying that she'd saved his life by having the phone installed."

"They sound like very special people."

"They were." Jacob swallowed hard, but he didn't look away from her. "I suppose that sometimes I forget the good memories...you know, trying not to dwell on the bad."

"I can understand that." Hannah thought of what her mother had said, that they'd both been dealt a blow.

Jacob cleared his throat and sat forward, arms crossed on the desk. "How do you know so much about accounting and IRS reports?"

"I first worked doing some accounting here in town, down at the furniture factory when I was a *youngie*."

"I didn't know that."

"You and I didn't stay in touch after our failed attempt at dating, not really."

"Maybe we should have."

"Why?"

She half hoped that he would answer, but he seemed suddenly interested in the snickerdoodle in his hand, so she let it slide.

"Okay, let's see what else I have here."

They went down her list of questions until

she felt like she had a fair understanding of his system—which wasn't much of a system, but at least it was consistent.

Finally she said, "This isn't going to be as complicated as I feared. You only have a few categories that your deductions will fall under. I am curious, though—how did you even pay your taxes without knowing exactly what you'd made and what you'd spent?"

"I tried to fill out the IRS worksheets, but mostly that was a guessing game. Mainly I looked at my balance in my bank account and paid based on that."

"But you must have spent money that wasn't business related."

"Look around, Hannah. Does it look like I've spent much on the place?"

"I see your point."

"No big vacations, no major purchases, it seemed pretty straightforward to me."

"Everyone has to file taxes—even Amish."

"Not if we make under a certain amount, and believe me, if I made over that amount, it wasn't by much."

"That's true for individuals, but businesses must file whether they have a profit or loss."

"Which I did."

"And yet you're being audited. Perhaps you

didn't include all the forms you were required to include."

When he looked at her skeptically, she explained, "After I married, I did my husband's taxes for the farm. We even had a nice Mennonite woman come to the local library and help us."

"*Wunderbaar.* Then you know what you're doing."

"Let's hope so." She tapped her pen against the pad.

"What?"

"You might have some money coming back to you. There are a lot of deductions that wouldn't have shown up as an extra expense. Like, say, the use of this part of the barn."

Jacob glanced left and right and then leaned forward. "You mean this room? I've heard it's small and stuffy and poorly lit."

She crossed her arms in defense, but she couldn't help smiling. "*Ya.* I think you're right. Still, it's deductible because it's the place you do business, as is the part out there where you work on your projects."

"You're *gut* at this, Hannah."

"Better wait until we're through the audit to decide that. Speaking of the audit…"

This time it was Jacob that groaned instead of the chair.

"We only have ten days, Jacob."

"Are you sure?"

"According to the letter they sent, an agent will be here to examine your files on September 10."

"Oh."

"Today is August 28."

"Can we ask for an extension?"

"We can, but…the Mennonite woman in Wisconsin, she had a college degree in accounting and worked for a local accountant. She said that the IRS will grant an extension, but they'll look at things more closely because of it. Also, any penalties you have would be greater because more time will have passed since you owed the taxes."

"I just want to build playhouses."

"*Ya*, most business owners love what they do, but they're not prepared for the amount of paperwork that comes with it."

"Can you have it ready? By the tenth?"

"Maybe, if I take it home with me, work on it a little each night and put in as many hours here as possible." Even as she uttered those words, Hannah wondered what in the world she was doing. She wanted to spend time with Matthew. She wanted to work in the garden. She didn't want to spend every free minute taping up Jacob's receipts.

"You would do that?"

"I guess, but is there anyone else who could help? Anyone who could at least tape these receipts onto sheets of paper for me? That would save a lot of time."

"I have five nephews who live next door. They're always bugging me to come see them."

"You don't go next door to see your nephews?"

"I've been busy is all." Jacob began gathering up their cups and putting the lid back on the empty Tupperware.

"How old are they?"

"Oldest is eleven, no…twelve."

"That's certainly old enough to help with this project, and my niece Naomi was looking for a way to earn a little Christmas money."

"Let's tell the *kinder* that I'll pay them two bucks an hour. Wait, will I be in trouble with the child labor laws?"

"I don't think taping receipts for an hour each night falls into that category."

*"Gut."* He stood, holding the cups in his left hand and tapping on the table with his right. "I'll load up one of the bins later today in your buggy for you to take to your niece."

"Load two. I'll work on one and Naomi can work on the other."

"And I'll take two over to my nephews."

"We need to get the past five years in order. Can you do the last one?"

Jacob shook his head in disbelief. "You're pushy, you know that?"

But the way he smiled at Hannah sent a river of good feelings through her.

Jacob turned to go back into the main room. As she worked she could hear him in there—humming and sanding, and occasionally using some sort of battery-powered tool. She felt a new optimism that maybe they could be ready in time. It would take a tremendous effort, but she'd never minded hard work.

And with the extra overtime hours, she might just be able to help save her parents' farm.

As for Jacob, it wasn't as if they were friends, but it felt good to have an employer she could talk to. It helped to know that he'd forgiven her for her behavior the day before.

Despite the silly schoolgirl feelings she sometimes had around Jacob, she also understood that she was a mother and her sole focus was her child. She wasn't interested in dating or expanding her social circle. Still, they could learn to enjoy working with one another—as long as they kept things on a professional basis, she saw no harm in it.

To be professional one needed to extend certain courtesies, so perhaps her mother was right. Maybe they both needed to work on their social skills.

## *Chapter Eight*

Jacob had fallen into a comfortable routine by Thursday afternoon. On days that Hannah left early to take Matthew to therapy, he would putter around in his workshop until she arrived. Then they'd spend thirty minutes talking about what progress they'd made on the accounting reconstruction, whether she had any questions and if he'd thought of any other items she needed to know about his business.

His excuses for being there were relatively lame—needing to put a final coat of sealant on a birdhouse, giving his gelding Bo time in the pasture, not wanting to get caught in early-morning traffic.

On the days when she didn't leave early, he was gone before she arrived. He did this so he could be at the job site early, finish his work well before four and come home in time to spend the last hour or so with Hannah. They didn't work together. He was usually in the workshop, and she was in the tiny office. But just knowing someone else was there seemed to give the old barn new life.

His schedule was set, and he was pretty happy with it.

He left for work late on therapy days—Tuesday, Wednesday, and Friday. He left for home early on Monday and Thursday. He always had an answer ready in case anyone asked, as if he needed to justify his irregular hours.

He didn't share his excuses with Hannah. Instead he recited them to himself over and over in his mind.

He should be there in case she had questions.

He needed to catch up on his small jobs.

She might need something moved in the office.

But with each day that passed, he understood that those were just excuses. *You might be able to fool someone else part of the time, but you can rarely fool yourself.* The memory of his father's words brought a smile as he made his way home early Thursday afternoon.

Deep inside, beneath all the layers of why it wouldn't work and how foolish he was being, Jacob understood that he was falling for Hannah.

It was hard to believe that she had been working in his office for less than a week. It seemed like she belonged there.

Thursday he arrived home around two o'clock. His days on the job site were getting shorter and shorter, but the boss was happy with what he'd been able to accomplish, and that was what mattered.

He'd opened the large doors of the barn to let in the fall air and was working on a front entry bench for one of his *Englisch* neighbors when Hannah plopped into a chair next to his workbench.

"Problem with the receipts? Let me guess, you can't tell my threes from my eights."

"*Nein*. It's not about the numbers."

"What is it? Is Matthew okay?" He clutched the piece of sandpaper he'd been using in both hands. Surely she would have told him if Matthew wasn't well.

"He's fine. It's only that he's turning five in a couple of weeks."

"When is his birthday?"

"September 25."

"We should have a party."

Hannah crossed her arms, as if to ward off more unwelcome ideas. "Matthew prefers to have small, private celebrations."

Matthew did? Or Hannah? He was about to ask when common sense saved him and he closed his mouth. It wasn't his business how she raised her child, or at least it shouldn't be. Should it?

"But that's not what I came to tell you. I'm going to need to leave early today, even though it's not a therapy day."

Jacob pushed away the disappointment that welled up inside him. "That's not a problem."

"You're sure?"

"*Ya.* I know you're doing extra work at home. From the stack of pages on your desk it would seem the great taping project of the year is nearly done."

"Speaking of taping…how's your bin coming along?"

Instead of admitting that he hadn't actually started, he asked, "Why do they have to be taped up anyway? A receipt is a receipt."

Hannah's eyes widened and she looked at him as if he were wearing two pairs of suspenders. "Because the IRS doesn't deal in scraps of paper, and when I enter them in the ledger, I do so by date."

"You have to sort them by date?"

Hannah shook her head in mock despair, or maybe it was real despair. "Stick to your woodwork, Jacob Schrock. Leave the office work to me."

He liked the sound of that. He liked the idea that she planned to stick around longer than the next two weeks.

Hannah went back into the office, ignoring the way that Jacob was looking at her. Maybe she was imagining it, but he seemed happy when she was around, almost as happy as he had been when he was working on Matthew's playhouse.

She plopped down in front of the desk. She was helping him out of a jam. Of course he was happy. Why wouldn't he be happy? Things weren't that clear-cut, though. She understood all too well that he was helping her out of a jam at the same time.

She'd taken the most recent year of receipts herself, and she'd stayed up well past her normal bedtime—sitting at the kitchen table, taping receipts and sorting them by month. Now, back in Jacob's office, she opened the journal and began entering them under the proper category headings. She immersed herself in the work, and thirty minutes later was surprised to hear the clatter of buggy wheels outside.

Looking up, she saw that it was her brother-in-law and began tidying up the desk. She'd brought a quilted bag from home, and she carefully placed the next two months of receipts in it, along with the ledger, a few extra pencils and the battery-operated sharpener she'd purchased at the store.

By the time she'd made it out into the larger room, Jacob was wiping his hands off on a cloth and frowning at the buggy that had parked in front of the workshop.

"Your ride?" he asked.

*"Ya."*

He nodded once, curtly, and turned back toward his workbench.

"I'm taking some work with me, to make up for the time I'm missing." When he didn't answer she added, "Thanks again, Jacob."

He bobbed his head but was suddenly completely focused on cleaning some of his tools. It all seemed like rather odd behavior. Usually Jacob was the friendly, outgoing sort.

Shrugging, she said, "See you tomorrow, I guess."

Still no answer, so she gave up on making conversation and walked outside.

Her brother-in-law had just pulled up to the hitching post and jumped out of the buggy.

"Carl, *danki* for picking me up."

"No problem."

"When *Dat* dropped me off, he thought he'd be able to come back and get me."

*"Ya*, he told me as much, but his errands in

town took longer than he thought. It's really no problem, Hannah."

He put his arm around her shoulders and gave her a clumsy hug. Carl was the big brother she'd never had. He'd been in the family over a dozen years, and Hannah thought the world of him. It helped that he was so good with Matthew, who happened to be sitting in the back seat practically bouncing up and down, if a boy with a spinal cord injury could bounce.

Hannah stuck her head inside. "What are you doing here?"

"Carl said I could come."

"And why would you want to do that?"

"I told you, *Mamm*. I want to see where you work. Is Jacob here? Can I come inside?"

"Oh, I don't think we have time for that."

"Sure we do," Carl said. "I even brought his chair."

Hannah resisted the urge to ask why in the world he would do that. Carl was just trying to help, and Matthew's fascination with Jacob hadn't lessened one bit in the last few days. She didn't think this was a good idea, but Carl was already removing Matthew's wheelchair from where it was strapped on the back of the buggy.

"All right," she said with a sigh. "Let's get this over with."

\* \* \*

Jacob had immediately gone to the window when Hannah walked out of the room. He knew he shouldn't be aggravated with her. He couldn't expect her to work all of the time, and of course she had a social life. Why wouldn't she? Hannah was a smart, beautiful, young woman. She'd been a widow for over a year now. Of course she was lonely and ready to step out again. He was surprised she didn't have beaus dropping her off and picking her up every day.

When the man jumped out of the buggy and gave her a hug, Jacob understood the full depth of his misery. Not only had he fallen for a woman who could never possibly care for an ogre like himself, but she was already being courted. He could have asked around. He could have saved himself the embarrassment.

He thought to sneak out the back and over to his house or the garden or anywhere that he wouldn't have to watch the two of them when the man walked around to the back of the buggy. He reappeared with Matthew's wheelchair. She had trusted Matthew with this fellow? They must be even closer than he feared.

Now he was torn, but that feeling didn't last long because the man had plopped Matthew into the chair as if he weighed no more than a sack of potatoes. Matthew was grinning up at his mother, and Hannah was pointing at the workshop. There was no way he was going to sneak out of this. He wasn't beneath slipping away and being borderline rude to an Amish man, but he couldn't find it in his heart to ignore young Matthew.

So he pulled in a deep breath, straightened his suspenders and walked out into the fall afternoon.

Matthew let out a squeal the minute he saw him.

"Jacob! Carl brought me over to see where you work."

Hannah reached forward and straightened Matthew's shirt. "I thought he came to pick me up."

"That too." Carl stepped forward and offered his hand to Jacob. "It's been a while."

A while?

"We were in the same church district, before we grew too big and had to split."

He did look familiar.

The man laughed good-naturedly. "Carl Yoder. I'm married to Hannah's sister, Beth."

The flood of relief that swept through Jacob confirmed what he had already figured out— he'd developed feelings for Hannah King, and he was in much too far to back out now.

He spent the next twenty minutes walking Carl and Matthew through the workshop, showing them the types of things he made and answering Matthew's endless supply of questions.

"I want to see your playhouses, Jacob."

"You have one of my playhouses, buddy."

"But I want to see the other ones. The ones that you made for other people. Are they all for disabled kids like me?"

"Yes, they are, but different kids have different special needs."

"I don't know what that means."

"Some disabilities you can see on the outside, but others, they're inside—so those playhouses might not have grab bars. Maybe the person can't see well, so the playhouse is flat on the ground—no steps and no ramps."

"How's that a playhouse, then?"

Jacob laughed and ruffled the hair on the top of Matthew's head.

"Say, isn't there one over by me?" Carl asked. "Built like a ship. That has to be your work."

"*Ya.* Made it last year for a young boy with cancer."

"Can I see it?" Matthew began tugging on his hand. "Can we go there? Would he let me play with him?"

"I'm not sure how Jasper is doing now. We'd need to check with his parents."

"Will you? Will you call them?"

"That's enough, Matthew." Hannah had moved behind Matthew's chair and had pivoted it toward the barn door. "Jacob has lots to do. He can't be ferrying you around to playgrounds because you're curious."

"I could take you both on Saturday."

Matthew squealed in delight and raised his hand for a fist bump. Jacob obliged and then he noticed the frown on Hannah's face.

"Oh. Unless you had something else you needed to do on Saturday."

"I had planned on working on your receipts."

"We could go without you. I don't mind taking him."

"You need to work on receipts too."

"Well, we could do that in the morning and go to see the playhouse in the afternoon."

"Come on, *Mamm*. Please…" Matthew drew the word out in a well-practiced whine, but he added a smile, which caused his mother to sigh heavily.

"Okay, but only for an hour."

"Jacob could come for lunch and then we could—"

"Let's not strain your *mamm*'s patience. She has things planned for her Saturday."

Carl had been studying a row of birdhouses. He picked one up and asked, "How much?"

"Ten."

"Costs you more than that to build it."

"*Nein.* I use old barn wood. Costs practically nothing to build it."

Carl grinned. "I'll take two, then. Beth will love them."

Matthew offered to hold the birdhouses, and Carl once again shook Jacob's hand. "This has been great, but I need to get back before Beth thinks I've taken off for the auction in Shipshe without her."

"I didn't know you were going," Hannah said.

"She wants goats, if you can believe that. As if she doesn't have enough to take care of, and the new baby on the way..." Carl shook his head as if he couldn't fathom the ways of women and offered to wheel Matthew back to the buggy.

Hannah hung back, and Jacob had the feeling that it wasn't to say *thank you.*

"I'm sorry he pressured you into that."

"It's not a problem."

"A four-year-old can be quite persistent once they've made up their mind, and Matthew doubly so. He's been pestering me about coming to see you since I started on Monday."

"I really don't mind."

"The thing is..." Hannah hesitated and then pushed on. "Matthew gets attached to people and then they move on to other…phases of their lives. He doesn't handle that very well."

"Where would I move on to?"

"He gets too attached, if you know what I mean."

"I don't." He waited, wondering what she did mean and trying not to be stung by her suggestion that he was going to somehow let Matthew down.

"It's up to me to protect him."

"From what? *Freinden?*"

"You're not his *freind*, Jacob."

"Of course I am."

"*Nein.* You're my boss."

He stared out the window for a moment, watched Carl lift Matthew out of his wheelchair and place him in the buggy. He wondered how hard it was for Hannah to depend on other people, especially after losing her husband. "Let me take you both out on Saturday, show him a couple of playhouses. We'll keep it to an hour so it doesn't disrupt your whole day."

"Okay, fine. I guess."

"I know the owners, and they wouldn't mind Matthew playing on them. Most are for children his age."

"Playdates don't always go well with Matthew."

"What do you mean?"

"Other children can't possibly understand his limitations, why he needs to be careful…"

"I've worked with several disabled kids. They seem pretty intuitive about such things."

"And I've seen children point and ask cruel questions, or, worse yet, ignore him completely."

"Is that what you're worried about? Or is it that you're afraid I'll somehow let Matthew down? Because I can assure you right now that isn't going to happen."

"He's too taken with you."

"Excuse me?"

"He doesn't understand that you were simply hired to do a job, and that now I'm hired to do a job. He thinks…well, he thinks that there's something more to it."

"Hannah, what you're saying is true, or was true. I was hired for a job, and now I've hired you for a job." He wondered if he should just shut up, but ignored that idea. "I think, though, that Matthew is also right. We're part of a community. We belong to the same church."

"Different districts."

"We are neighbors and *freinden*."

She nodded once, curtly, and turned. He walked beside her as she made her way back outside. Carl had climbed into the buggy and was waiting.

He'd noticed that when she was embarrassed

or nervous, she liked to keep her hands busy. At the moment, she was twisting the strings to her prayer *kapp* round and round. He'd also learned that if he waited, she would eventually work through her emotions and pick up the conversation again.

"*Ya*, of course you're right. It's only that I don't want him to get the wrong idea."

"What wrong idea? That I like you? Because I do."

She cocked her had to the side, glancing up at him and allowing her gaze to linger there before flitting away. "We'll see you Saturday, two o'clock."

And then, she scurried back off to the buggy. There was simply no other word for it. She reminded him of a squirrel running back toward its safe spot in the woods.

The question was, how he was ever going to convince her that being with him was safe and that they were more than friends. Were they? Or was his imagination running wild again? He reached up to scratch at the scars on his face.

Scars.

Everyone had them, but his were hideous. He'd thought that keeping them, that refusing the cosmetic surgery, would help pay the debt he owed for not saving his parents. He'd never considered that they might push away someone that he cared about. What if Hannah simply couldn't abide looking at him from one day to the next? She'd never hinted at that, but people could hide their feelings. If she was repulsed by him, it wouldn't mean that she was shallow, only that she was human.

He walked back into his workshop and began sanding again, more aggressively this time.

He didn't know if Hannah was worried about protecting Matthew's feelings or her own, but he did know that she needed to stop shielding the boy from all of life's ups and downs. Matthew needed friends the same as everyone else, and if it meant that someone occasionally let him down…that was part of growing up.

One other thing he knew for certain. He wouldn't be the one to disappoint Matthew. Now all he had to do was find a way to convince Hannah of that.

It was risky. Putting his feelings out there would mean that he might be hurt, and he'd had his fair share of that already. But not letting her know how he felt? Not taking a chance to get to know her on a personal level? That felt like a bigger risk than he was willing to take.

# Chapter Nine

Friday dawned beautiful, cool and crisp. If she'd lived closer, Hannah would have walked to work. As it was, she said goodbye to her family and drove Dolly the few miles to Jacob's place. She was still uncomfortable with the way things had ended between them the day before. Had he actually said he liked her? What did that mean?

Fortunately he wasn't there when she arrived, so she didn't have to worry about being embarrassed about the way they'd left things. She went straight to the office and was soon immersed in receipts and columns of figures and IRS categories. The morning passed quickly and her stomach began to grumble. She was about to pull over yet another box of receipts when she heard a whistle from out in the yard. She hurried to the door and saw Emily Schrock making her way toward the workshop, a basket over her arm and a smile on her face. Hannah hadn't seen Jacob's sister-in-law in years. In fact, the last time she'd seen her they'd been in grade school together.

"Tell me you have some cold tea or hot coffee in there."

"I have both, and scones too—fresh blueberry."

Emily was nearly as round as she was tall, and she always had been as far back as Hannah could remember. She was the traditional Amish woman, and probably could have starred in one of the local Amish plays. Quick with a smile, an excellent cook and, if Hannah remembered right, she had a whole passel of children. As Emily stepped closer, Hannah realized she was also expecting another child, though her baby bump wasn't yet too obvious. It seemed Hannah's lot in life to be surrounded by pregnant women.

"Come in the office. I finally finished cleaning."

Emily let out a long whistle as she walked into the room. "Wow. You did all of this...this week?"

Hannah allowed the woman to enfold her in a hug.

"We're so glad you're here."

"We?"

"Micah and I. We worry about Jacob, and the

IRS audit… Micah was ready to hire one of the *Englisch* accountants in town."

"He may still need to. I haven't actually worked through all of his receipts yet."

"And his books?"

"He doesn't have any."

"I suppose that's part of the problem. I'm sure you'll be able to fix it, though. I remember how you were in school. Math was your favorite subject."

"Still is," Hannah admitted. "It's what I enjoy about quilting, the measuring and calculating."

"And what I always make mistakes on. How about we go outside? The rocking chairs looked more comfortable than the stool you have behind your desk."

Hannah readily agreed. As they walked back out into the fall sunshine, she asked, "How are you? I see you're expecting again."

"I am, and I dearly hope it's a girl, though of course we'll love whatever *Gotte* blesses us with." She opened the thermos and poured two cups of coffee.

It was much better than what Jacob made in the workshop, and Hannah sipped it with pleasure, closing her eyes and enjoying the rich taste.

"You have several boys already, right?"

"Five. Samuel is twelve. He's our oldest. The

twins—Timothy and Thomas—are ten. Eli's nine, and Joseph is six."

"I'll never remember all those names." Hannah laughed and plucked one of the scones from the basket.

"You know how it is with Amish families—big and loud and messy." As if suddenly remembering Hannah's situation, she set down the scone she'd been eating and brushed off her fingertips on her apron. "I was so sorry to hear about Matthew's accident, and your husband... a real tragedy."

*"Danki."* The word was barely a whisper.

"I should have come to see you."

*"Nein.* Why would you? You have your hands full with your own children and husband to care for, your home to maintain and—"

"Why would I?" Emily looked truly shocked at the question. "Because we're *freinden.* Because we take care of each other, like family."

Nearly the same words that Jacob had said to Hannah earlier.

Emily picked up her scone and finished it off with the last of her coffee. "I know we're not technically in the same district, but that doesn't matter. We're still one community. Maybe you could bring Matthew to meet my boys."

"Oh, I don't know—"

"They're rambunctious but they're *gut* boys."

"Where are they at this morning?"

"With my parents, who live on the other side of us. They'll all be in school this year. My youngest is only a year older than Matthew. He's four, right?"

"Nearly five."

"And Joseph is barely six. They could be *gut frienden*."

Hannah didn't answer that. She thought it unlikely that a healthy six-year-old would want to be friends with a disabled five-year-old. The thought stung her, stirred the old ache, and she pushed it away.

"Tell me about Jacob," she said, more to change the subject than anything else.

"Oh, *ya*, sure. There's not a lot to tell. You know about the fire."

"My mother told me about it."

"Happened six years ago, but he still hasn't healed from that night, in my opinion."

"He was here when it happened?"

"*Nein.* He was downtown, courting a young girl from the next district. He came back late and the home was already ablaze."

"Lightning is what *Mamm* said."

"So the firefighters told us. Jacob blames himself, I think."

"For a lightning strike?"

"More because he wasn't here. He didn't get to

them in time, or he might have saved them—at least that's what he said when they were transporting him to the hospital. Maybe he blames Micah too. Our place is next door but over the hill. We didn't realize what had happened until we heard the fire trucks."

"Jacob ran into it...into the fire?"

"He did." Emily began tidying up, offered Hannah another scone, then repacked the picnic basket. "His scars—the ones on the inside—they are far worse than the ones on his face."

"It must be hard—being disfigured."

Emily shook her head so hard that her *kapp* strings swung back and forth. "No one even notices anymore. What they see is what he is—a *gut* man who is hurting."

Hannah realized Emily was right; she hadn't really thought of his scars in a long time. She certainly didn't notice them anymore. "And yet it's hard to be different."

"Not if we're humble, it isn't."

Hannah bit back the retort that came too quickly to her lips. *What would you know of being different?* It was often easy for those not suffering from a thing to tell you how to handle it. She didn't utter either of those thoughts aloud, however. Emily obviously cared for Jacob and only wanted what was best for him.

Hannah set her chair to rocking, determined

not to butt into the other family's affairs. Emily, however, wasn't done yet, perhaps because she had no other woman in her household to share her worries and concerns with.

"I know several *gut* women who would be happy to court Jacob, but he can't see past his own scars. It worries me, for sure and certain it does."

"You care about him."

"All I know to do is keep trying, because if you ask me, Jacob needs a family. He needs to get his attention off himself and onto someone else. He needs to learn to love again."

Friday didn't work out the way Jacob had hoped. He had to be at the job early, before sunrise, so that he could finish the cabinetry work in time for the job superintendent to approve what he'd done. He could have pushed some of the work off until Saturday, but he had plans with Hannah and Matthew the next day. That thought had him whistling through his breakfast of oatmeal and coffee.

He finished the cabinetry job well before lunch. He told himself that he didn't work quickly so that he could at least say hello to Hannah before she left for Matthew's appointment, but in truth he wanted a glimpse of her. Somehow seeing her each day improved his mood, even if it was only to have her shove a scrap of paper into his hands and say, "Can you explain this one to me?"

The job site manager grinned as he checked off the boxes on his approval form. "Hot date, Jacob? I've never seen you work so fast."

"Some orders are backed up in my shop is all."

Which was a true statement, if not completely honest. Or was it completely honest? There was no real reason to be at the shop with Hannah. She seemed to be doing fine on her own.

"Uh-huh, well, as usual you've done an excellent job. Sign here." The man thrust a clipboard toward him. "Your payment should be processed early next week."

*"Danki."*

"Thank you, and I'll be needing you for that job in Shipshewana mid-September, if that still sounds good to you."

"Sounds great."

But the thought of riding the construction firm's bus to Shipshewana each day didn't appeal to him as it once had. The truth was that he'd rather be home.

Still, the cabinetry work allowed him to spend time on the playhouses, and he'd received another order for one the day before. He was itching to get to his workshop and work on a design plan. The little girl had cerebral palsy. Her form said that she loved anything pink, sparkly or related to Princess Belle. He'd had to ask a co-worker what that last one meant.

*"Beauty and the Beast?* Surely you've seen it."

When Jacob shook his head, the man had said, "Come to my house. My littlest watches it at least once a day."

So instead of going straight home at noon on Friday, he stopped by the library and used the computers to find a short description of the movie. Pulling out a scrap of paper from his pocket he'd written:

*bright, beautiful, young woman.*

*beast lives in castle.*

*he has a good heart and she loves to read.*

Not a lot to go on, but those three lines were enough. Suddenly he knew what he wanted to build. A castle with bookcases and one of those giggle mirrors that was both safe and fun. He'd seen them on a school playground he'd helped build. In fact, if he remembered correctly, the construction manager had ordered it from the local hardware store.

He walked from the library to the store, ordered the mirror and set off toward home. It was only a little after noon, so he should get there before Hannah left for the day. He'd hardly spent any time with her, but he had peeked into the office each evening. It smelled and looked better, and he had to admit that her changes to the room made a lot of sense. She seemed to be making progress, based on the stacks of taped receipts and notations in the spiral notebook she'd bought. She'd even begun to write in the accounting book he'd purchased.

He arrived a few minutes after noon to find Hannah and Emily sitting in the rockers underneath the porch of the workshop.

"Any scones left for me?" he asked, dropping down onto the porch floor.

Emily peered into the basket. "Looks empty."

"I know you are teasing me, Emily." Jacob pulled the basket out of her hands, dug around inside the dish towels and came away with a giant oatmeal cookie. "This will do."

"You're in an awfully *gut* mood."

"Why wouldn't I be? Finished my job early. The check is in the mail, and I get to work on a new playhouse this afternoon."

"Who is this one for?" Hannah asked.

"Young girl here in town actually. She has cerebral palsy. It's a disease that—"

"I know what it is," Hannah said softly. "CP affects muscle tone, posture, even eyesight."

"The poor thing." Emily poured Jacob a mug of coffee from her thermos and handed it to him. "Any idea what kind of playhouse you're going to build?"

"Apparently she likes some *Englisch* movie called *Beauty and the Beast,* so I'm thinking it should be in the shape of a castle, complete with turrets, bookcases and a funny mirror. That's my initial plan, anyway."

"It will be *wunderbaar*, Jacob." Emily began storing items back into her basket. "I better get home. The boys went to town with Micah, but they'll be back soon."

"I hope my *bruder* and my nephews appreciate you and your cooking abilities." Jacob finished the cookie and snagged the thermos of coffee before she tucked it away. "Sure there aren't more cookies in there? I'm still hungry."

"Because you need to eat real food, not just sweets. Speaking of hungry…don't forget brunch on Sunday."

"Oh, I…"

"Jacob Schrock, you will not be working on Sunday, and since there's no church, I expect you to be at our house by ten thirty in the morning."

Jacob glanced at Hannah, a smile tugging at his lips. "My sister-in-law can be quite bossy, if you haven't noticed."

"You should listen to her."

"I should?"

"Sure. She's a *gut* cook and your nephews apparently don't see you very much."

"Now, that makes me think you two have been talking about me."

Emily stopped what she was doing and studied Hannah, her head cocked. "You should come too."

"Me?"

"Bring Matthew. He can meet the boys."

"Oh, I don't think—"

"And your parents. I haven't seen Claire and Alton in ages."

"I'm sure they have other plans."

Emily ran a hand over her stomach, then placed the basket over her arm and smiled at Hannah. "Just ask them. We'd love to have you."

With a small wave, she set off across the property to her house.

"You two do this every day?"

"I've only been here a week. This is actually the first time Emily has stopped by."

"It's *gut* she did. Emily doesn't get enough girl time according to Micah. I suppose living with a house full of males could try anyone's patience."

But Hannah wasn't listening. She'd dumped the contents of her coffee mug onto a nearby plant, repositioned the rocking chairs and headed back inside without another word.

Jacob followed her, suspecting something was wrong but clueless as to what it might be.

"It would be great if you and Matthew could

come Sunday…and your parents too, of course. Emily usually has a small-sized group—enough to get up a game of ball, but not so many that the buggies are crowded together."

Hannah definitely wasn't listening. She'd practically run into the office, and now she was perched on her stool pulling yet another stack of receipts toward her.

"Hannah? What's wrong?"

"We won't be coming on Sunday."

"Oh. I just thought Matthew might enjoy—"

"You don't know anything about what Matthew might or might not enjoy." Two bright red spots appeared on her cheeks, but her gaze remained on the receipts, which she was now pulling out haphazardly. "Meeting new people is very hard for him."

"For him…or for you?"

"That's not fair."

"Oh, really?"

"Yes, really." She jumped off the stool, nearly toppling it over in the process. Hands on her hips, she said, "It's easy enough for you to boss me around, but when was the last time you were at your *bruder*'s house?"

"That's not the point."

"Isn't it? You're telling me that it's *gut* to be together, but apparently you stay here in your workshop whenever possible, hiding away."

"I'm not hiding." His temper was rising, and he fought to keep his voice down. "It's true I've been busy, but I don't avoid seeing them, and you shouldn't avoid introducing Matthew to new people."

"Why would you say that?" All color had drained from her face. "Why would you pretend to know what I should or shouldn't do?"

"I worked with Matthew on the playhouse. I know he's lonely."

"You know nothing! You haven't seen him on Sundays, longing to do what the other children do, but confined to his chair."

"I'm sure that must be difficult for you."

"You don't hear him cry when he has a terrible dream or when he's wet his bed because he can't get up by himself."

"I wasn't saying—"

"You know nothing of our life, Jacob Schrock, and I'd thank you to stay out of it."

With those words, she pushed past him, hurried across the main room of the workshop and dashed into the bathroom, slamming the door shut behind her.

Hannah managed to avoid Jacob for the next hour. When it was time for her to leave, she would have walked through the main workroom without speaking, but Jacob called out to her before she reached the door.

"If you'd like to cancel tomorrow, if you'd rather not take Matthew to see the playhouses, I understand."

She was mortified that she'd actually hollered at him. He'd been nothing but kind to both her and Jacob, and she'd responded with accusations and bitter words. So instead of jumping on his offer, she murmured, "*Nein.* We'll see you at two o'clock."

She was feeling so miserable about the entire situation that she found herself confessing to Sally Lapp as she waited for Matthew to finish his PT appointment.

"I shouldn't have said those things, but he made me so angry."

"Which is understandable, dear."

"What does he know of raising a child like Matthew?"

"Some people are like buttons, popping off at the wrong time!"

"Now I don't know if you mean me or Jacob."

"Perhaps both."

"Plus we're spending an hour tomorrow with him. Did I tell you about our plan to go and see his playhouses?"

"*Ya.* Sounds like a nice afternoon out."

"But seeing him both days of the weekend? It seems a little much..."

Hannah had brought a stack of the receipts with her and was beginning to enter them in the ledger. She looked down at what she'd done. Her handwriting was a tight, precise cursive and her numbers lined up perfectly, but seeing the progress she'd made on Jacob's accounts didn't ease the guilt she felt.

"I'll need to apologize to him."

"We often feel better after we do."

"And I will, even though he's wrong. Matthew does not need to be thrown into new situations."

"Mothers often know best."

"He's barely had time to settle in from the move, get to know his cousins and *aentis* and *onkels*, not to mention his new church family..."

"And yet children are ever so much more resilient than adults." Sally had finished the blanket she'd been working on the week before. Her yarn was now variegated autumn colors.

It reminded Hannah of cool nights and shorter days.

"So you think we should go to Emily's on Sunday?"

"Oh, it's not important what *I* think. What is your heart telling you to do?"

Hannah stared down at the column of numbers, embarrassed that tears had sprung to her eyes. Why was she so emotional? Why did she feel the need to run from Jacob Schrock? And what was she so intent on protecting her son from when he was thriving?

"Sometimes I'm not sure," she admitted.

"Pray on it. Make a decision when you're rested, not in the middle or at the end of a long, hard day. Maybe talk to your parents."

The door to the waiting room opened, and a nurse pushed Matthew's wheelchair through.

"*Gut* day?" Hannah asked.

"Awesome day."

He pestered her about Jacob all the way home—wanting to know if she'd seen him, what he was working on, what he'd said about their plans to visit a couple of his playhouses the next day. Hannah realized as they pulled into the short lane leading to her parents' home that it wasn't only Matthew she was trying to protect. She was also trying to protect herself.

Raising any child was difficult, but raising a special needs child presented issues she'd never imagined. She constantly felt on guard for his feelings as well as his personal safety. She didn't think she could handle Matthew's look of disappointment when the other children ran off to play, or the whispered comments when no one thought she was listening or the looks of pity as she pulled his wheelchair from the buggy.

Life was difficult.

The one thing that made it easier was being home, alone, where the eyes of the world couldn't pry. She only guessed that it made things easier for Matthew, but she was certain that it made things easier for herself.

Hannah needn't have worried about making a decision as to whether they should join Jacob's family for Sunday dinner. Emily had spoken with Hannah's mother when they saw each other at the grocer in town. Plans had already been set in motion.

She had no valid objections, so she didn't bother to argue, but the entire thing made her tired and cranky. She had hardly slept Friday night after her argument with Jacob, and Saturday she worked twice as hard around the house—trying to make up for being gone all week. By the time they'd set lunch out on the table, she was tempted to beg off, say she had a headache, stay home and take a nap.

One look at Matthew told her that wouldn't be possible. He was wiggling in his chair and tapping his fingers against the table.

During the meal Matthew peppered her with questions about the playhouses, and when she'd said *I don't know* to over a dozen questions, he moved on to asking her about Jacob's family.

"Do they have animals?"

"I'm sure they do."

"Sheep?"

"Why would they have sheep?"

"Camels?"

Hannah began to laugh in exasperation, but her father combed his fingers through his beard as if he were in deep thought. Finally he leaned toward Matthew and lowered his voice as if to share a secret. "Only Amish man I know in this area with camels is Simon Eberly over in Middlebury. I'm sure I would have heard if Jacob's family had any—so no, probably not."

Which only slowed Matthew down for a moment. He proceeded to fire off questions about camels and declare that he'd love to have one. When Hannah thought her patience was going to snap, her father took Matthew outside to see to the horses.

"He'll be fine, you know." Her mother started washing the dishes, which meant it was Hannah's turn to dry.

"Why do you say that?"

"It's plain as day you worry about him."

"Of course I worry."

"He'll be in school this time next year."

"Unless I hold him back a year. With his birthday being in September, we could decide to wait..."

"He's such a bright young boy. Already he's better with his letters and numbers than you girls were at that age. Why would you want to hold him back?"

"I don't know, *Mamm*." Hannah was tired, and she wasn't yet halfway through the day.

The time inched closer to two o'clock, and finally her mother suggested she might want to freshen up a bit.

Hannah waited until she'd left the room to roll her eyes. Freshen up? It wasn't a date. They were driving around to look at playhouses. She'd switch out of her cleaning dress, but she was not donning a fresh *kapp*. She certainly didn't want Jacob to get the wrong idea.

Then she remembered her conversation with Sally Lapp about the way she had treated Jacob. She'd made up her mind then, and she wasn't going to change it now. She needed to apologize to Jacob, and the sooner the better. Suddenly what she wore seemed much less important.

Jacob made sure he arrived exactly at two o'clock.

He'd apparently pushed a little too hard the day before. He hadn't even known that he was pushing, but the way Hannah had melted down told him that he'd touched on a very sensitive subject. He wanted today to be fun and relaxing, not stressful. So he was careful not to arrive early or late.

Which meant that he had to pull over on the side of the road and wait a few minutes before turning down the dirt lane that led to her father's house.

He needn't have worried about being early. Matthew and Hannah were waiting on the front porch. The sight of them—her standing behind his wheelchair, and Matthew shading his eyes as he watched down the lane—caused Jacob's thoughts to scatter, and for a moment he couldn't remember why he was there. Then he glanced over and saw Matthew's playhouse. "You're getting old, Jacob. Or daft. You could be growing daft."

Ten minutes later they were off.

The first stop was Jasper's house. The boy wasn't Amish, but he was sick. For three years now he had been valiantly fighting the cancer that threatened to consume his small body. Though nearly nine years old, he was approximately the same size as Matthew.

"Wanna see my boat?"

"*Ya.* I have a train."

"Did Jacob make it?"

"He did."

"He's *gut* at building things."

Jasper's mom explained that she needed to

stay inside with the baby, who was sleeping. "But make yourself at home. I was so glad to hear from you, Jacob, and Hannah, thank you for bringing Matthew. Jasper doesn't have a lot of visitors."

After walking her around the playhouse, which was built in the shape of a sailboat, Jacob pointed to a bench a few feet away. "Care to sit?"

"*Ya.* We cleaned all morning, so I'm tired."

"I heard you're working on a big accounting job during the week."

She laughed, then pressed her fingers to her lips.

"It's okay to laugh, Hannah. You're allowed."

"Oh, am I, now?" She tucked her chin and gave him a pointed look. He raised his hands in mock surrender, and she shook her head, then sighed.

"Do I exasperate you?" he asked.

"*Nein.* It's only that I need to do something I don't enjoy doing."

"Now?"

"*Ya.*"

"I'm intrigued."

"I need to apologize, Jacob." She glanced up at him and then away—toward the sailboat, where Jasper was showing Matthew how to hoist a miniature sail. "I was rude to you yesterday, and I'm very sorry. I know better than to speak harshly to someone, let alone someone who is being kind to us."

"It's my fault. I stuck my nose where it didn't belong."

Now she laughed outright, causing the boys to look over at them and wave.

"Perhaps you did, but it was probably something I needed to hear."

"Apology accepted."

*"Danki."*

*"Gem gschene."*

The moment felt curiously intimate, shared there on the bench with the sun slanting through golden trees. Jacob cleared his throat and tried to think of something else to say, but for the second time that day, his mind was completely blank.

"It's a fine line," Hannah said. "Giving him the extra attention and care his condition requires, but not being overly protective. I'm afraid I'm still learning."

"You're doing a *wunderbaar* job. Don't let any fool neighbor or cranky boss tell you different."

Which caused her to smile again, and suddenly the tension that had been between them was gone. He was tempted to reach for her hand or touch her shoulder, but he realized that what Hannah was offering with her apology was a precious thing—her friendship. For now, he needed to be satisfied with that.

* * *

Hannah felt herself softening toward Jacob. How could she resist? He was patient with Matthew, kind toward her and it was plain that he was a good man. They stopped at three different playhouses—Jasper's sailboat, a precious miniature cottage built for a young blind girl named Veronica, and a tiny-sized barn made for an Amish boy named John.

"I spoke with John's parents. They said we could come by and look, but that they wouldn't be here."

"Is he sick too?" Matthew asked.

"Not really sick, no, but he needed a special playground nonetheless."

"What's wrong with him?"

"John was born with only one leg. His left leg stops at the knee. It's a bit hard for him to get around at times."

"He uses crutches?"

"He does, and he wears a prosthetic."

"Prophetic?"

"*Nein.* A…" He glanced at Hannah, obviously hoping for help.

"It's a plastic leg, Matthew. Remember the older gentleman you see at physical therapy sometimes? He has one."

"But his is metal. I know because he let me

touch it. Looks like a robot. He laughed when I told him so."

"John's is plastic, but I've seen the metal ones." Jacob resettled his hat on his head. "It bothers him sometimes, and he likes to take it off when he gets home. The challenge for me was to make him a playhouse where it was safe to do that."

"This was a fun trip, Jacob. You're a *gut* builder."

"Thanks, Matt."

Jacob's use of a nickname that only her father and her husband had used melted another piece of Hannah's heart.

After they'd visited the small barn, Jacob drove them to town, bought ice cream for everyone and laughed with Matthew as they chased swirls of pink down their cones. It was all Hannah could do to remind herself as they drove home that this was an outing for Matthew, that it had nothing to do with her and Jacob, and that he was not interested in dating her.

Who would want a widow with a disabled child?

She knew how precious Matthew was, but she also understood firsthand the trials, the terrible nights, the emergency hospital visits, the mountain of bills. No, it would be wrong to consider letting anyone share such a burden. A preposterous thought, anyway. Jacob had been nothing but friendly toward her. Yes, he had said *I like you*, but that could be said of the neighbor's buggy.

Raising Matthew was a road that she was meant to travel alone.

When they reached the house, she went to transfer Matthew from the buggy to the chair, but Jacob was there to do it for her. His hand brushed against hers and then his brown eyes were staring into hers, searching her face, causing her hands to sweat and her heart to race.

As they thanked Jacob for the afternoon and she pushed a very tired young boy into the house, she paused to glance back over her shoulder. Jacob Schrock was a good man, and there was no doubt in her mind that *Gotte* had a plan for him, a plan that more than likely included a wife and family.

A whole family.

One that wasn't carrying the weight of her baggage.

## Chapter Ten

Sunday morning dawned crisper and cooler than the day before. Jacob owned two Sunday shirts—they were identical in size, color and fabric. So why did he try on the first, discard it, try on the second and then switch back to the first?

He studied his face in the mirror. If he turned right the reflection was of a normal man—not particularly good-looking, strong jawline, dark brown eyes, eyebrows that tended toward being bushy. If he turned right, he saw his father staring back at him.

But if he turned left, he saw in his scars the detour his life had taken—the pain and the anger and the regret. He saw what might have been.

It had taken him some time to learn to shave over the scars. Their Plain custom was for unmarried men to be clean shaven, so he worked the razor carefully over the damaged tissue, using his fingers more than his eyes to guide the blade.

Finishing, he tugged the towel from the rack and patted his face dry. He could lie to himself while he was sanding a piece of oak or shellacking a section of maple wood, but for those few moments each day when he faced his own reflection in the mirror, he saw and recognized the truth.

He was lonely.

He longed to have a wife.

He dreamed of a family and a real home.

There was a small kernel of hope buried deep in his heart that those things were possible.

The moment passed as it always did, and he finished preparing for the visit next door to see his brother's family.

He chose to walk and wasn't too surprised when the only one to meet him was his brother's dog, Skipper. No one had been able to figure out exactly what kind of mutt Skipper was, though there was definitely some Beagle, Labrador and Boxer mixed in his background somewhere. Jacob bent down to scratch the old dog behind the ears and then together they climbed the steps to the front porch. Skipper curled up in a slat of sunlight, and Jacob let himself in.

His brother's voice let him know the family was still having their devotional in the sitting room.

"'Therefore I am troubled at his presence; when I consider I am afraid of Him. For God maketh my heart soft, and the Almighty troubleth me.'"

"That doesn't make any sense." Samuel, the oldest of his nephews, sat on the far end of the sofa. Next to him were the twins, Tim and Thomas, then Eli, who was younger by eleven months, and finally Joseph, the baby of the group at six. All five nephews were lined up like stair steps.

"Why do you say that?" Micah asked, nodding at Jacob, who pulled a chair from the kitchen and took a seat.

"*Gotte* loves us." Samuel craned his neck and stared up at the corner of the ceiling as if he might find answers there. "The Bible says so. Remember? We read it just last week."

"*Ya*, that's true," Emily said.

"But Job is…what did you read?"

"He's afraid of *Gotte*," Eli piped up.

"Maybe Job did something wrong," Tim said.

"*Ya*, like when we get in trouble, and we know what we did was wrong and we're afraid of you finding out." Thomas pulled at the collar of his dress shirt. "Like last week when I put that big worm in the teacher's desk. It was awfully funny, but I knew even when I did it that I'd pay for it later."

"Sometimes we're afraid because we know we've sinned," Micah agreed. "But think back to the beginning of our reading this morning."

Micah thumbed through the pages of the old Bible—one of the few things they'd been able to recover from the fire. The cover was cracked and singed in places. The pages retained a slightly smoky odor, but it still held the wisdom they needed. Perhaps that Bible was like Jacob. It had been through a lot, but *Gotte* was still able to use it. *Gotte* was still able to use him.

"'There was a man in the land of Uz, whose name was Job,'" Micah read. "'And that man was perfect and upright, and one that feared *Gotte*.'"

Samuel shook his head. "Still doesn't make sense."

"Maybe your *onkel* Jacob can explain it better than I can."

Jacob met his brother's gaze, then turned his attention to the boys lined up on the couch. The five of them were so young to be learning the hard truths of life, and yet it was his and Micah's and Emily's jobs as adults, as elders in the faith and as the boys' family, to prepare them for such things.

Jacob understood what his brother was asking.

He thought of that morning, of the reflection in the mirror of two different men—only there weren't two different men. His scarred self didn't exist in isolation from the whole. He was one person, and if he believed the truth in the Good Book his brother was holding, then he needed to accept the person *Gotte* had created him to be.

Clearing his throat he sat forward, elbows propped on his knees, fingers interlaced. "Job loved *Gotte*, as we do, *ya*?"

All five boys nodded in unison.

"But his experiences had taught him that *Gotte*'s plan for his life might be painful, might be hard to understand at times. Those plans had him scarred and hurting, and so he was afraid."

No one spoke, and Jacob knew that they were waiting, that his family had been waiting for him to reach this point a long time—for six years, to be exact.

"It's a hard thing to know that bad things can happen to us, like the fire that took *Daddi* and *Mammi*."

"They're in heaven now." Joseph swung his foot back and forth, bumping the bottom of the couch.

"*Ya*, they are."

"But you're still scarred." Eli touched the left side of Jacob's face.

"I am scarred," he admitted. "And I have to

accept that somehow *Gotte* still has a plan for me, that what happened—that it wasn't a mistake. After all, *Gotte* could have sent a rainstorm and put out that fire…right?"

*"Ya."* Thomas, the practical one, crossed his arms. "I don't get it."

Jacob's laughter surprised everyone, including himself. "I'm not sure that we have to *get it*, but we do need to keep the faith, whether we understand or not."

They joined hands then, heads bowed in silent prayer, until Micah spoke aloud and asked the Lord to bless their day. The moment he said *amen*, the twins were headed out the door, Eli pulled a book out of his pocket and began to read it, and Micah asked for Samuel's help with setting things up for the luncheon. Joseph muttered something about a pet frog and hurried toward the mudroom.

It was Emily who held back. Standing on tiptoe, she planted a kiss on the left side of Jacob's face. Her stomach was rounded with her sixth child, and she had to lean forward to kiss his cheek. For a moment, Jacob thought he felt the life inside of her press up against him.

"What's that for?" Though he was embarrassed, he couldn't stop the smile that was spreading across his face.

"Just glad to see you is all." But the tears shining in her eyes told him it was more.

He patted her on the shoulder. Even he knew that pregnant women were emotional. He didn't want to be the cause of starting the waterworks before everyone arrived.

He needn't have worried, though. She was humming a tune as she waddled into the kitchen. It was only as he was left standing in the sitting room alone that he realized the song she was humming was "Amazing Grace."

By the time Hannah and Claire were done with the breakfast dishes, Hannah's father and Matthew were in the sitting room, waiting. Their devotional was from Christ's Sermon on the Mount.

Her father patiently answered Matthew's questions and then they all prayed for a few minutes. The devotional time reminded Hannah of her childhood, of sitting with her sisters, squirming on the couch much as Matthew was now squirming in his chair.

It took another hour to pack up the dishes they were taking for the luncheon, along with any special items Matthew might need. The weather was warm for the first weekend of September, and there was no chance of rain, which made it a perfect day for a Sunday social. They had to drive past Jacob's place to reach Emily's.

Matthew pointed out the workshop to his grandparents. "That's where *Mamm* works. I saw it, and Jacob took me around to look at his projects."

He rode in the back seat with Hannah and had his nose pressed to the buggy window. "Why can't we go there?"

"Because lunch is at Emily's," Hannah explained for the third time.

"And Emily is Jacob's *schweschder*."

"*Ya*. She married Jacob's brother, Micah. That makes them *bruder* and *schweschder*."

Matthew had more questions, but they were pulling into Emily and Micah's drive, and their buggy was suddenly surrounded by boys as well as an old gray dog.

Before Hannah had a chance to protest, her father had loaded Matthew into his wheelchair and Emily's boys had taken off with him across the yard.

"Maybe I should go…"

"He'll be fine," Emily assured her. "Come and have a glass of lemonade. It's warm out today, *ya*?"

She introduced Hannah to her parents and two more couples who were neighbors. They spent the next twenty minutes drinking lemonade and talking about crops and school and the general state of things in Goshen. Hannah was pretending to pay attention, but trying to catch sight of Matthew. Emily's boys had whisked him away, and she hadn't even had a chance to explain how to set the brake on the chair or what to do if he stopped breathing.

That last thought was ridiculous.

Why would he stop breathing?

But he might, and she hadn't explained what to do.

She excused herself from the group of adults and made her way over to the trampoline where Emily's twins were practicing flips. No sign of Matthew there. Hurrying toward the barn she spied the two oldest boys throwing horseshoes. Matthew wasn't watching that either. Which left the youngest boy—Joseph. Her son's life was in the hands of a six-year-old.

Her heart thumped and her palms began to sweat as she hurried toward the barn. Two thin lines in the dirt assured her that Matthew's chair had been pushed in this direction. She practically ran into the barn and slammed straight into Jacob.

"Whoa, there. Something wrong?"

"It's Matthew…" She glanced up at him, remembered his fingers brushing her arm the day before and glanced away. "I've been looking for him. I was worried that—"

"Just breathe, Hannah. Matthew is fine."

"Are you sure?"

"*Ya.* Come with me. I'll show you."

Jacob led her through the main room of the barn and toward the area where Micah kept his horses.

He reached the last stall and stopped, motioning for her to tiptoe toward him. They both peered around the corner.

Joseph was picking up a newborn kitten and setting it in Matthew's lap.

"I can hold him?"

"Sure."

"But what if I—"

"You won't."

"Are you sure I won't hurt him?"

"Look, he likes you."

The cat's cries subsided as Matthew bent over the small furry bundle in his lap.

"He's purring," Matthew said.

"*Ya.* He's happy."

"And the momma cat doesn't mind?"

"Probably not, for a minute or so at least."

They proceeded to discuss the merits of the different kittens—stripes over solids, large over small, loud over quiet. Jacob tugged on Hannah's arm and pulled her away from the stall. They walked out the side door of the barn into a day that was more summer than fall. Perhaps because he'd been in the barn the colors seemed brighter, the breeze sweeter. Or maybe that was due to the woman standing beside him.

He stepped to her left so that the right side of his face would be facing her. Then he realized what he'd done and felt like an idiot, as if he could impress her with half of his face. He hadn't been particularly good-looking before the fire.

They walked away from the barn, and he steered Hannah toward Emily's garden. The vegetables had all been harvested, but the flowers were a sight to behold.

"When Emily first married Micah, she couldn't keep a tomato plant alive. She'd spend time with *Mamm* in the garden every afternoon, and I guess some of *Mamm*'s gardening skills rubbed off on her."

"This is beautiful."

They walked up and down the rows and finally stopped at a bench.

*"Danki,"* Hannah said.

"For?"

"For taking me to him."

"You were worried."

"For inviting us here."

"That was really Emily's doing."

"For being our friend."

"Of course I'm your friend, Hannah."

Instead of answering, she became preoccupied with her *kapp* strings, running them through her fingers again and again.

Finally he said, "Tell me about David."

Her eyebrows arched up in surprise. "My husband?"

*"Ya."*

"You mean how he died."

"I heard about that, and I'm sorry."

She glanced away, but she seemed more surprised than offended so he pushed on.

"I meant more what was he like? I know he was from the Shipshe district, but I only met him once or twice, both times at the auction."

"He was a *gut* man."

"I'm sure he was."

"I miss him."

"Of course you do."

Hannah smiled and chuckled softly. "He wasn't perfect, though. He thought Wisconsin was the promised land. We moved there only a few months after we married."

"And was it? The promised land?"

"In truth it was remote, and the Plain community there was different. I won't say it was worse, but it took some getting used to. One half allowed for gas appliances, even solar energy.

The other? They were more Old Order, at least in practice."

"I've heard about the ice fishing there."

"*Ach.* The winters were incredibly difficult. We had more than forty inches of snow each of the winters I was there."

"That much?"

"*Ya.* It was very different from here."

"Were you happy—living in this promised land?"

"We were."

"That's *gut.*"

"I haven't spoken of him, for a while. You know how it is in a Plain community."

"We believe his life was complete."

"Yes." Her voice grew softer so that he had to lean toward her more to make out her words. "I want Matthew to know about his father. He might not be old enough to have his own memories, but I want to share mine."

"You're a *gut mamm.*"

She shrugged her shoulders. "Some days I wonder about that."

There was a racket across from them and then Matthew and Joseph tumbled out of the barn, Joseph pushing as fast as he could and then jumping on the back of the wheelchair as if it were a bicycle. Matthew's laughter carried across to them.

"I should go and see if he needs anything."

"Does it look like he needs anything?"

She laughed then. "I suppose you're right."

"I want to show you something."

He led her down the path to the other end of the garden.

"Why have you never married?" Her hand flew to her mouth and her eyes widened. "That was rude of me. I shouldn't have asked."

"It's nothing my family doesn't ask me every chance they get."

"They worry about you."

"I suppose. Emily and Micah, they think because they're happy that everyone should be married with a houseful of *kinder*."

"And you don't want that?"

"I don't know. It would take a special person to be able to put up with me."

"Because of your scars?"

"Partly."

"But they're only...scars."

Jacob glanced at her and then away. "I don't really see them anymore. Sometimes I forget and look in the mirror and I'm surprised. Or a child sees me, say an *Englischer* in town or a new family in our community, and they point or ask questions..."

"Curious, I suppose."

"Yes, but it reminds me that my face is frightening to some people."

"Surely it's not as bad as all that."

Jacob didn't argue the point. She couldn't know what it was like to live his life, to see the looks of revulsion on people's faces.

"This is what I wanted to show you." He led her under an arbor with a thick vine covering it. A path wound through clumps of butterfly weeds with bright orange flowers sitting atop three-foot stems. Back among the taller blooms on a piece of board taken from an old barn, someone had painted the names of his parents and placed it into the ground like a street sign.

"It's how we remember them."

"You have a garden at your house too."

"*Ya.* Not as well tended as Emily's, but we both make an effort to spend time in them. It's our way of being sure my parents' memory stays with the children."

"It's nice here. I like it."

"*Mamm* loved her garden. She sometimes needed time away from two rambunctious boys. *Dat* would tell us to clean up the dishes, and he'd head out to the garden with a cup of hot tea for her. I'd find them there sometimes, holding hands, their heads together like two *youngies*."

"That's a special memory, Jacob."

"It is."

"Thank you for sharing it with me—for showing me this."

"You're welcome. I'm glad you and Matthew were able to come today."

And then he did something he wouldn't have believed that he had the courage to do. He stepped forward, touched Hannah's face until she looked up at him and softly kissed her lips.

She froze, like a deer caught in a buggy's headlights.

Blushing a bright red, she stepped away, stared at the ground, looked back at him and finally said, "I really should see if he needs me."

Jacob nodded as if he understood, but as she was hurrying back over to the picnic tables, it seemed to him that she wasn't actually running toward Matthew. It was more as if she was running away from him, and could he really blame her? What had possessed him to think that she would enjoy a stroll through the garden with him?

What had prompted him to kiss her? Perhaps that had been a mistake. It wasn't something he could take back, though, so he straightened his suspenders and headed over to where the boys were playing horseshoes.

Hannah didn't breathe freely until she was sitting among the women, listening to them discuss the best fall recipes. She wasn't thinking about pumpkin-spice bread or butternut squash casserole, though. She was thinking about her son holding a kitten, about the fact that he had a new friend, about the garden and about Jacob.

She was thinking about that kiss.

When he'd spoken about his scars, she'd had an urge to reach out and touch them, to assure him that they all had scars.

She'd wanted to tell him that she had scars too.

Her heart probably looked worse than his face...it was only that people couldn't see those scars. She kept them hidden. She smiled and pretended everything was fine.

She pretended through the meal as she made sure that Matthew ate.

She pretended as she watched Matthew go off again, this time with Emily's entire clan of boys.

She pretended while the women circled up and spoke of the upcoming school auction.

"I'm growing old and forgetful," her mother said. "I meant to clean out my casserole dish before the leftover potatoes become as hard as concrete."

"I'll get it, *Mamm*."

"Oh, I didn't mean for you to do that."

"It's not a problem." She was actually relieved to be away from the group of women, though she'd run toward them before the meal. Still, an hour spent in their presence and her cheeks hurt from trying to smile. She was happy for an excuse to spend a few minutes alone.

She retrieved the dish from the table, took it into Emily's kitchen and rinsed it out.

As she scrubbed away at the residual cheese, her thoughts returned to Jacob—to doubts and questions and scars and hurts.

She was thinking of that, of how some hurts showed physically while others remained concealed when she stepped outside and practically collided with Elizabeth Byler.

"Hannah. Could you help me with this?"

Hannah made a practice of avoiding Elizabeth, who she remembered from her youth. Elizabeth was a negative person with a nasty habit of gossiping, but the woman was holding a large tray filled with used coffee mugs.

It would be rude to run away.

"Of course. Let me hold the door."

"Emily was going to leave this out in the sun, covered with flies. Best to get them in and cleaned."

"Oh…"

"If you'll wash, I'll dry."

Hannah smiled her answer, since there seemed to be no way to avoid spending twenty minutes in the kitchen with the woman.

She'd barely run soapy water into the sink

when Elizabeth started in on what was obviously her agenda.

"Saw you walking off with Jacob."

"*Ya*, he wanted to show me the garden."

"You're not the first."

"First?"

"Probably won't be the last."

"The last to what?"

"Set your *kapp* on Jacob Schrock, which is why I thought it my job to warn you."

"Warn me?" Hannah stared at the woman in disbelief.

"That road goes nowhere. You're wasting your time with that one."

Hannah felt her temper rise. She tried to focus on the mug she was filling with soapy water, but the buzzing in her ears was a sure sign that she was about to say something she'd regret.

"Give it a month, at the most two, and you'll be crying on someone's shoulder about how your heart is broken. Best to listen to sense. No disrespect to Micah, but his *bruder* Jacob is spoiled goods."

Hannah's hands froze on the mug she was washing. "Surely you don't mean that."

"Don't look at me that way, Hannah. You know better than anyone what it's like to live with a person who has been damaged. Would you want Matthew married to someone?"

"Excuse me?" Hannah dropped the mug into the water, causing suds to splash up and onto her sleeves.

"Don't get me wrong. *Gotte* has a plan for every life."

"Nice of you to admit that."

"Jacob's tried dating a few times, but it didn't work out. He has quite the chip on his shoulder. I will admit that financially he's certainly a catch since he inherited that farm from his parents."

"So now he's a catch?"

"Some women think so."

"Elizabeth, I don't know what to say."

"You could thank me for speaking the truth. I'm only trying to help you see straight."

"That's very kind of you."

"Wisdom, Hannah. It comes with age. You'll see. Think about it. What woman would want to wake up to a disfigured husband every morning?"

"That's uncharitable, Elizabeth."

"Not to mention that Jacob feels sorry for himself, as if he's the only one who has troubles."

Hannah gave up on washing the mug, dropped it into the sudsy water and carefully dried her hands on a dishrag. She attempted to count to ten but only made it to three.

"I think I'm needed outside."

"It won't be the first time I'm left to do dishes by myself."

"Maybe that's because you're a bitter, unpleasant person."

Beth's mouth opened into a perfect *O*, but no sound came out.

"I'm sorry. I know your life has been hard too, with Jared's drinking problem and all…"

"I do not want to talk about Jared."

"But your personal trials don't give you a reason to speak ill of Jacob—"

"I did not."

"Also, I'd appreciate it if you'd refrain from determining the course of my son's life when he is but four years old." And with that, Hannah turned and walked back out into the afternoon sunshine, feeling better than she had in a very long time.

It wasn't until she was on her way home in the buggy that she allowed her mind to comb back over Elizabeth's harsh words. Her parents were speaking quietly in the front, and Matthew had fallen asleep with his head in her lap. She was brushing the hair out of his eyes, thinking of what a beautiful and kind child he was, when Elizabeth's words came back to her as clearly as if the woman were sitting beside her in the buggy.

*You're not the first.*

*Probably won't be the last.*

*Financially he's certainly a catch.*

There were women in their district interested in Jacob? Well, of course there were. That shouldn't surprise her one bit, and it certainly wasn't any of her business.

She had no plans of dating the man, despite the kiss. That had been an impulsive thing for him to do. Somewhere deep inside she'd known he was going to. She should have kept her distance. What had she been thinking?

She worked for him. She wanted to help her parents and to provide for Matthew. She didn't need to step out with anyone. She had no intention of doing such a thing. If Elizabeth thought so, that was her misunderstanding.

Jacob was a friend, a neighbor of sorts and her employer. He was nothing more, and though she might defend him to nosy interfering women, she had no intention of falling in love with the man. Her heart had suffered enough damage, or so she told herself as the sun began to set across the Indiana fields.

## Chapter Eleven

The next week passed quickly. Jacob managed to finish the bin of receipts that he'd been assigned, as had his nephews and Hannah's niece. If he managed to survive this audit, it would be because they'd worked together.

He peeked into the office as often as he dared, and slowly Hannah managed to create order out of his chaos. She'd asked him to find a filing cabinet, and earlier in the week he'd spied one that had been set out in the trash by a local Realtor. After checking to be sure it was free, he strapped it to the back of his buggy, brought it home, cleaned it inside and out, and oiled the tracks the drawers ran on.

"Could use a new paint job, but I suppose it will do."

"It's perfect." Hannah had already purchased a box of folders and the next day she transferred the taped-up receipts to the file drawers—chronological, three years per drawer, orderly and neat.

He hoped the IRS agent would be impressed. He certainly was. The bins were stacked in the corner of the room and when they were all empty, he carried them to the stall he used as a storage place.

Hannah beamed as if she'd baked the perfect apple pie. She was proud of her work, as she should be. He thought again of the bonus he meant to give her, almost said something, but decided to wait. If he owed money to the government, he would need to meet that obligation first. It would be wrong to suggest she might receive extra money for her labor and then disappoint her.

But he wanted to raise her hopes, to ease the worry he saw in her eyes. How much money had her sisters and parents been able to raise? He spoke to her again about approaching her bishop and asking for help, but she only shook her head and said something about *humility* and *Gotte's wille* and *stubborn men*.

Every time he saw her, he thought of the kiss they'd shared.

Hannah, on the other hand, seemed completely focused on the audit. It was after lunch on Friday when she finally admitted, "I think we're ready."

The office barely resembled the place it had been before Hannah came to work there. A bright yellow basket of mums sat next to a pot of aloe vera. The afternoon light splashed through the sparkling panes of glass. Hannah's sweater was draped across the back of the new office chair he'd purchased and the shelf held her quilted lunch bag. She opened the bottom drawer of the desk and pulled out her purse.

"So you're headed home?"

"*Ya.* Matthew has therapy today."

"Of course. How's he doing?"

"*Gut.* Getting stronger, I think. It helps that he's able to have the same therapist every time he goes."

She stood there, waiting, as Jacob's mind jumped back and forth looking for something else to say. He wasn't ready for her to leave, but he realized he looked like a fool, standing there silently and twirling his hat in his hands. He crammed it back on his head and said perhaps too gruffly, "*Danki* for your help."

"Of course. It's what you hired me for."

"*Ya*, but we both know you've gone above and beyond. I don't know if we'll pass the audit or not, but if we do, it's because of you."

"And your nephews and my niece."

"*Ya.*" The same thought he'd had earlier. It was almost as if she understood his thoughts.

She blushed prettily then, and he nearly asked her out to eat or to go for a buggy ride or perhaps hire a driver to take them to Shipshe. But she was already gathering her things together, talking about a cousin from Pennsylvania who was coming into town and how she needed to help her *mamm* prepare.

It seemed her weekend was full of plans, so he wished her a good afternoon and pretended there was a rocker he needed to finish working on.

There was a rocker he needed to work on— and a dresser, a coffee table, as well as plans for a playhouse later in the month. He tried working on each one, but he couldn't seem to find the right sandpaper, or varnish or idea. Finally he gave up, harnessed Bo to the buggy and headed toward town.

Jacob was standing in line at the library and thought the woman in line ahead of him was Hannah. He made a fool of himself calling out to her only to have the stranger look at him oddly and hurry off.

His gelding, Bo, seemed full of energy, so Jacob decided to head north of town and scout the area where he'd be building a playhouse for a child with Down syndrome. He thought he passed Hannah on the road and his heart rate accelerated and he waved his hand out the window, but it wasn't Hannah. Of course it wasn't. Matthew's therapy appointment was in the middle of town, not on a country road headed north, plus the horse he'd just waved at was a nice roan and Hannah's horse was chestnut.

He even convinced himself that it was her buggy parked in front of his brother's house. When he pulled in, with the excuse that he'd promised his nephews he'd come by and pick up one of the kittens, he found it was one of the older women from the next district who'd stopped by to drop off two bags of clothes for the boys. Too late—he either had to admit he'd made up the excuse or go to the barn and pick out a kitten.

The boys gave him the black one with white patches around its eyes.

"Don't forget to feed it." Tim looked concerned.

"Of course I'll feed it."

"Do you even have cat food?" Thomas asked.

"No. I don't have a cat."

"You do now." Samuel reached forward and scratched the kitten between the ears. "We'll loan you some until you get to the store."

Joseph ran off to fetch a container.

Jacob tried to stifle the groan, but without much success.

"Didn't know you were in the market for a

cat, *bruder*." Micah stood grinning at him, as if he too could read his mind.

"I've been wrestled into this."

"*Ya*, my *kinder* are quite convincing."

"And don't leave him in the barn alone, Jacob." Eli looked at him with the seriousness only a nine-year-old could muster. "Are you sure you don't want two?"

"I'm not sure I want one."

"Then put him in your mudroom. He needs to be able to hear you so he won't be scared."

His trailer didn't have a mudroom, but Jacob decided not to point that out. Perhaps he could make a place for the kitten next to his washing machine, or in the office. Wouldn't that be a nice surprise for Hannah? The IRS agent might not appreciate it, so perhaps he'd wait until the end of the audit. In the meantime, he'd try to find out whether she even liked animals.

He whistled as he drove back toward his house, realizing that he'd made it through Friday. Two more days to stumble through and then Hannah would be back at her desk.

"It's *gut* when family comes to visit, *ya*?" Hannah's mom slipped a cup of coffee in front of her.

Matthew was in bed.

Her father was checking things in the barn.

And the weekend was finally over.

"*Ya*, it is."

"Only…?"

"I wasn't about to add anything else."

Her mother sipped her coffee, studying her over the rim of the cup.

"I suppose I was thinking about the audit tomorrow," Hannah said.

"Are you ready?"

"I've done my best."

"Then you're ready." Her mother reached forward and patted the back of her hand.

When Hannah looked down and saw that, her mother's hand on top of hers, something stirred in her chest. Too often she took her parents for granted, took her life for granted. What would Jacob give for just one more hour of sipping coffee with his parents?

"And now I've upset you."

"*Nein.* It's only, I was thinking of Jacob and how awful it would be to lose your parents."

Her *mamm* sat back, reached for a peanut butter bar, broke it in half and pushed a portion of it toward Hannah. "No one lives forever."

"I know that."

"Not that I'm in a hurry to die."

"I should hope not."

"You're thinking of this all wrong."

"I am?"

"It's true that Jacob is lonely, and that he's looking for his way in life."

"He's lonely?"

"But as for his parents? Don't mourn them, Hannah. They are resting in the arms of *Gotte*, dancing around his throne. What we see dimly they see clearly now."

Hannah couldn't help laughing. "I guess when you put it that way…"

"Now tell me about Jacob."

"About him?"

"Has he kissed you yet?"

*"Mamm!"*

"You don't have to share if you don't want to."

Hannah changed the subject. They sat there for another half hour, speaking of relatives, the coming fall and Matthew's birthday. What they didn't discuss sat between them. Though Hannah wanted to ask about the amount they owed the bank and how they were progressing toward meeting that debt, she didn't want to ruin this moment on a Sunday night, sitting in the house she'd grown up in. She didn't want to think about where they might be in a month or a year. She wanted to close her eyes and pretend, just for a moment, that everything would be fine.

Hannah and Jacob stood shoulder to shoulder, staring out the window as the small green car pulled down the lane. It stopped well shy of the parking area.

"What's she doing?" Hannah stepped closer, practically rubbing her nose against the glass.

If anything, she seemed more keyed up than Jacob felt.

He attempted to ease her nerves by putting a hand on her shoulder, but she jumped as if he'd stuck her with a hot poker.

"It's going to be fine," he said.

"*Ya*, but what's she doing? Who stops in the middle of a lane?"

"Looks like she's on her phone."

"Maybe she thinks she can't use it in here."

"Or maybe she has an important call. Maybe there's an emergency audit that she needs to leave for."

Hannah bumped her shoulder against his. "Don't joke that way. We need this to be over."

"She's moving again."

The car stopped next to the hitching post.

"How can an *Englisch* vehicle be that quiet?"

"My guess would be that it's electric and expensive."

"Electric? So she has to…plug it in?"

"*Ya*, they have a large battery that holds a significant charge. You have to plug them in at night."

"What if you run out of..." Hannah twirled her finger round and round.

"Juice? There's a backup fuel supply like other *Englisch* cars use."

"How do you know all this?"

Jacob shrugged. They might be Amish, but they didn't live on the moon. Most men, Amish or *Englisch*, were interested when a new type of vehicle came out. He'd read a few articles on electric cars. He considered explaining that to Hannah, but she was already moving toward the door of the barn, so he squared his shoulders and followed her.

The *Englisch* woman looked to be in her early twenties. She had pale skin, spiky black hair and multiple piercings in both ears. Roughly Hannah's height, she looked more like a girl than a woman. She was dressed in a sweater-type dress that settled two inches above her knees and high-heeled leather boots. Jacob wouldn't have guessed her weight to be more than a hundred pounds.

She'd made it out of the car, but now she stood halfway between it and them, staring down at her phone, her thumbs flying over the mobile device. There was a swish sound and then she dropped it into her leather handbag and looked up at them.

"I'm Piper Jenkins, your IRS auditor. You must be Jacob."

"*Ya*, Jacob Schrock. Good to meet you."

She turned to Hannah, but then a buzz came from her purse. She reached into it and scooped out her phone. Rolling her eyes, she dropped it back into the bag.

"I'm Hannah King. I've been helping Jacob with his accounts." Hannah clasped her hands in front of her. She'd admitted earlier that morning that she was worried the auditor would question her credentials.

Jacob almost laughed at the look of relief on her face when Piper said, "Oh, good. I'm glad to hear that he has help. Many of the Amish men I've audited try to take care of accounting on their own, and that doesn't usually end well."

"It's certainly not something I excel at," Jacob said. "If you'd like to come inside, we've set up a place for you to work in the office."

Hannah had arrived a half hour early that morning, all in a frenzy because they hadn't thought to set up a work area for the woman. In short order, Jacob had dragged in a desk that he was working on for a client, Hannah had popped her chair next to the desk and he'd retrieved the stool that she had originally used.

"Are you sure you wouldn't rather have your old office chair?" He'd put it in the corner of his workroom and used it to stack items on. The new kitten, Blackie, had taken it over and turned it into her daytime napping spot.

"That old thing? I'm surprised it holds the cat. No thank you. I'll take the stool."

They'd pushed the desks so that the two women would be facing each other. It was crowded, but it worked.

Now Piper walked into the room, paused a moment and then nodded in approval. "Let's see what you've got for me."

It occurred to Jacob that he should be tense, but honestly he believed that he'd done right by the US Treasury Department. Perhaps he hadn't filed the correct forms, but he'd paid his fair share of taxes. He wasn't worried about the outcome, especially with Hannah at the helm.

She had saved him, in more ways than one.

He no longer rose each morning wondering what the point was, or went to sleep worried that the days stretched out endlessly in front of him. She'd done more than straighten up his accounting—she'd added hope and optimism to his life.

That thought was foremost on his mind as the two women began pulling out files and pencils and calculators and highlighters and rulers. He'd never been so happy to walk into the other room and pick up a piece of sandpaper in his life. He did not want to be anywhere near what was going on between those two, but he'd stay close just in case they needed him.

His fervent prayer was that they wouldn't.

"It's you and me, Blackie." The cat wound around his legs, purring and leaving a trail of black hair. Arching her back, she stretched, then flopped in a ray of sunlight.

"Uh-huh. Well, the rest of us have work to do."

Three days later, the audit was over.

"We're not allowed to recommend businesses to help with audits." Piper stole one last glance at her cell phone, typed something in with a flurry of her thumbs, then dropped it into her purse. She finished putting her pens, highlighters, computer and notepad into her matching designer backpack. Finally she glanced up at Hannah and seemed surprised to find her still there. "I'm sorry, what was I saying?"

"That you're not allowed to recommend businesses."

"Right. But there is a place on the Goshen Chamber of Commerce website to list your services, and I recommend that you do so. I see a lot of businesses, especially Amish businesses, that could use your organizational skills."

Hannah glanced up at Jacob, who was trying to hide a smile.

*"Danki,"* she said. She didn't add that she

wouldn't be listing her services. She had a job with Jacob, and she liked the work. Plus, he needed her. Left to his own devices he'd be stacking up bins of receipts again in no time.

A small buzz permeated the silence. Piper snatched the phone back out of her bag, typed again, smiled to herself, and dropped it back in before turning her attention to Jacob. "I hope you appreciate her."

"Oh, I do." He glanced at Hannah and wiggled his eyebrows.

She gave him her most stern look.

How could he play around with an IRS auditor standing in the office?

"You'll receive a letter within ten days stating that the audit has been closed." She glanced at Hannah, smiled and leveled a piercing gaze at Jacob. "You passed with flying colors, and the refund that you're owed will be applied to this year's bill, per your instructions."

She headed toward the door, then stopped and turned back toward them. "I want to thank you both for the work you do for children with disabilities. It's a very good thing, and I'm sure it brings much joy into their lives."

And then she was gone.

Hannah finally let out the breath that it seemed she'd been holding since Monday morning. "I wonder what she does on that phone."

"Same as writing a letter—at least that's what the *youngies* say."

"Who has that many letters to write?"

"Indeed."

"Makes me glad we don't have them."

"Oh? You don't want an *Englisch* cell phone?"

"I do not." She knew he was teasing and realized she shouldn't rise to the bait, but she couldn't help herself. "I'm the one who spent the last few days with Piper Jenkins."

"I was hiding in the workshop."

"I noticed."

"Can you blame me?"

"The woman couldn't finish a sentence without checking the screen of her cell phone at least once. Seems a complete waste of time to me." She sounded old, sounded like one of their elders who insisted that all change was dangerous. She didn't believe that, but she didn't know how to explain to Jacob what she was feeling and why.

So instead she turned her attention to pulling out her work for the day—the receipts Jacob had given her from the previous week. She knew he was still standing there, still watching her and it made her heart beat wildly and her palms sweat. Finally she looked up, met his gaze and tried not to return the smile.

She pretended to glance back down at her work. She was finding it harder and harder to maintain the distance she had sworn that she would put between her and Jacob. He'd somehow found a way to worm into her heart, slide beneath her defenses and scale the wall she'd built with such determination.

He reached into his jacket and pulled out an envelope. "This is the missing check you couldn't find."

"Oh."

"I wrote it a week ago."

"You did?"

"And I've been holding it for the right moment."

She glanced up now, and when she looked at Jacob she felt like she was leaping into a giant pool of water. Though she'd been terrified when he'd kissed her, today it seemed like the fear that had permeated her decisions and her emotions since the accident was gone. "Now is the right moment?"

"It is."

She took the envelope and stared down at her name in his familiar handwriting.

"It's for me?"

"*Ya*, it's for you, Hannah, because of how much help you've been."

"But you pay me a salary to be helpful."

"You've gone above and beyond. Believe me, I know that I couldn't have passed that audit without you. I'd have needed to hire one of the *Englisch* accountants, and that would have cost me much more than the amount of the check you're holding."

"Jacob…"

"Open it."

She turned it over, slipped her nail beneath the flap and opened the envelope. When she pulled out the check, when she saw the amount written there, she tried to thrust it back into his hands.

"I can't take this."

"Of course you can."

"It's too much."

"*Nein.* It's the right amount, and it was the right amount whether we passed the audit or not." He walked around, took the envelope and check from her, and set them on the desk. Then he reached for her hands. "I know you've been taking work home, working longer hours than you've been reporting."

"I wanted to be ready." She tried to still the trembling in her arms and resist the urge to look up into his eyes. She knew if she did, if she allowed herself to see the goodness and kindness there, that there would be no turning back.

Jacob's voice was soft, and he rubbed his thumbs over the backs of her hands. "And I appreciate that. The amount of the check, even with what I've been paying you, it's nowhere near what the accountant in town was going to charge me."

"But—"

"I want you to have it, Hannah. I want you to use it to help your father."

And those were the magic words that convinced her to pull her hands away from his, pick up the check and tuck it into her purse.

Her heart was hammering, and she was trying to remember what she was about to do before he'd offered her the envelope.

Jacob walked back to the door and had stepped into the main room, but he pivoted back toward her, still smiling. "I forgot to tell you that your *dat* called. He's going to be later than he thought and asked if I could take you home."

"You don't have to do that."

"It's a long way to walk."

He laughed and she realized what a handsome man Jacob was. She'd not really thought about it. Oh, she'd spent many hours thinking about how she felt around him, but not about his appearance. She understood as she studied him with the afternoon sun slanting across the floor that when she looked at Jacob she didn't see his scars anymore. They weren't who he was, they were simply a reminder of something that had happened to him and of how precious life really was.

"I need to go by the Troyer home. It's on the way to your place. Do you mind?"

*"Nein."*

"Leave in an hour?"

*"Ya.* An hour will be fine." She couldn't look at him any longer, couldn't meet those eyes that made her feel like she was falling. Instead she stared down at the receipts in her hand until she heard him walk away.

Then she collapsed into her chair and covered her face with her hands.

The audit was over.

They'd passed.

And hopefully she'd made enough money to help save her father's farm.

# Chapter Twelve

Jacob tried to focus on the bedside table he was working on finishing. It was a simple piece made from walnut wood, and he should have been done with it already. He opened the drawer, confirming that it slid smoothly along the grooves. Then he stood it up on his workbench and began cleaning it one final time. Some furniture makers used fancy cleansers, but Jacob preferred doing things the old way—a little dish soap in warm water worked fine.

Using a soft cloth, he went over the table's surface three times. He wanted to remove all dust particles before putting on the final coat. Thirty minutes passed, and he found he was still cleaning the piece. In fact, he'd been rubbing the cloth over the same side for several minutes.

Once he was sure it was completely dry, he would apply a final coat of beeswax on the piece, but what was he to do with the next twenty minutes while Hannah finished up in the office? The memory of how she'd smiled at him, of the look of gratitude on her face when she'd accepted the check, made his thoughts scurry in a dozen directions—directions his thoughts had no business going.

Because it wasn't possible that Hannah King was interested in him romantically.

But what if she was?

She hadn't exactly run away when he'd kissed her at his brother's. Okay, she *had* run away, but maybe because she was embarrassed or confused. It didn't necessarily mean she didn't like it.

He dropped the rag in disgust and walked outside.

Maybe fresh air would help to clear his head.

But the problem wasn't the stuffiness in the workshop or the table he'd been working on. The problem was admitting what he felt for Hannah.

He walked across to the garden, wandered down the path and stopped at a bench. Sitting down, he glanced around him, then hopped right back up. He needed to keep moving. He needed to settle the restless feeling that made his heart gallop like Bo running across a field. That was normal behavior for a horse, but he was a man and he should have better control of his thoughts and his feelings.

A butterfly landed on a white aster bush in full bloom and then a red bird hopped onto the path in front of him. He stood there, frozen, watching it. Red birds were his mother's favorite bird. Her voice came back to him in that moment—gentle, full of wisdom, full of love.

*A cardinal can be a special sign from your loved one in heaven.*

When he closed his eyes he saw both his mother and father sitting on the front porch, talking and shelling peas between them, when the cardinal alighted on the porch rail. He had walked up and laughed at them, told them they looked like two old folks sitting around rocking and gossiping. His father had smiled knowingly, but his mother had pointed out the red bird.

Jacob missed them more than he would have thought possible, even after all these years. They'd been good people and what had happened to them, it didn't make any sense to him.

It wasn't that he doubted *Gotte's wille* for their lives; it was only that he didn't understand why it had to cause such pain…why their lives had to be complete at that moment, why they couldn't have stayed and grown old together and met all of their grandchildren.

Walking on through the garden, he circled

back toward the workshop and saw the silhouette of Hannah working in the office. What would his mother think of her? Of Matthew? He knew the answer to both questions, and the knowledge of that caused him to laugh out loud. He'd turned twenty when his mother had begun to tease him about settling down and marrying.

*A plump wife and a big barn never did any man harm.*

*An industrious wife is the best savings account.*

*Marriage may be made in heaven, but man is responsible for the upkeep.*

They had never doubted that he would one day marry, that having a family was the life *Gotte* had chosen for him just as it was for his brother.

Yes, his mother would like Hannah and Matthew.

She would approve of the feelings that Jacob was struggling with.

Both his mother and his father would want him to continue on with his life, and in that moment he knew that it was all right for him to want a family, to want Hannah and Matthew. It was all right for him to move on from mourning his parents, and to finally let go of the guilt that he carried. He might not understand the path his life had taken, the scars and battles and fears that had consumed the last few years, but he understood where he was at this moment.

And he understood that it was time to step out in faith.

Hannah was quiet as they made their way down the road. She knew she should make conversation, but she didn't know what to say, and her mind kept going back to the bonus check.

Had she thanked him properly?

Should she try to do so now?

But Jacob was talking about the weather and seeing a red bird, and the school auction and picnic coming up on Saturday.

"Well?" he asked.

"Well, what?"

"Your thoughts were drifting."

"*Ya*, I suppose they were."

"I was asking if I could take you to the picnic...you and Matthew."

There were a dozen reasons she should say no, but she heard herself say, "*Ya*, Jacob. That would be nice."

He looked as surprised as she felt.

Grinning he resettled his hat on his head. "*Gut*. I'll be by at eleven on Saturday."

Had she just agreed to go on a date with Jacob? What would she wear? What was she thinking? Was it a date if Matthew was going along? How would she explain to her son that they were just friends? How was she ever going to make it through the workday tomorrow without dying of embarrassment each time he walked into the office?

She couldn't date her boss!

He directed the mare to turn down a lane, toward a house that Hannah had never been to before. It was technically in Jacob's district, and it was newer so it hadn't been there when they were children, when the two districts were one.

"Judith and Tom moved here a few years ago. Their daughter's name is Rachel."

"She's the little girl with cerebral palsy?"

"Right. She's eight, loves to read and is fascinated with any story about princesses."

They found Judith Troyer in the garden behind the house, pulling the last of the produce from her garden. She wore a drab gray dress and a black apron. Her hair was pulled back so tightly that it puckered the skin at the edge of her *kapp*.

Jacob introduced her to Hannah and then said, "The giggle mirror arrived. I was hoping I could install it, if you don't mind."

"Of course I don't mind. *Danki* for bringing it over."

Which was when Hannah noticed the small figure in a wheelchair sitting in what looked like a castle's turret, though it was actually only a couple of feet off the ground. Hannah longed to go and look at the playhouse, to see what Jacob had done, but she felt rude leaving Judith, who had returned to harvesting the few remaining carrots, snap peas and tomatoes.

"May I help?"

Judith looked her up and down and finally shrugged. "Suit yourself."

The house wasn't poor exactly. Hannah picked up a basket from the gardening supplies and moved up and down the rows of vegetables. She kept glancing at the single-story home, the garden, the yard. She tried to put her finger on what was missing.

She pulled off a large bell pepper, a lovely deep red with a rich green stem, and glanced back at the house. That was it. There was no color. No flowers in pots or beds or the garden.

Everything was utilitarian.

No toys scattered around the yard. In fact, the only color came from the playhouse. Jacob had somehow found pink and purple roof tiles which he'd fastened to the top of the turret along with a small flag that waved and crackled in the slight breeze.

"Jacob told me about your son," Judith said.

"Oh. Matthew. *Ya*, Jacob built him a playhouse too. It's how we met—how we met again.

We attended school together many years ago, but now my family lives in the next district."

"If you ask me, the playhouses are foolishness."

"Excuse me?"

"A waste of *Englisch* money. I would have told the foundation no, but Tom…" She waved a hand toward the barn. "Tom thinks it will help her, as if a playhouse could do such a thing."

"I'm sorry…about Rachel's condition."

"Not your fault." Judith dropped to her knees and began digging up potatoes. Each time she'd find one, she'd shake it vigorously, as if the dirt clinging to its roots offended her, and then place it in her basket with a *tsk* of disapproval.

"Matthew has enjoyed his playhouse. He can spend hours out there, pretending and reading and enjoying the sunshine." She hadn't realized what a blessing the playhouse was until that moment, until she felt a need to defend it to this woman.

"And what good does that do?"

"Pretending?"

"That and playing…"

"Surely children need to play."

"Acting as if all is well when it isn't and it never will be again."

"So our children shouldn't enjoy life? Because their futures are…" She almost said *bleak*, but she didn't believe that. She thought of Matthew's smile, his quick wit, his loving personality. She thought of his legs, withered and useless. Like Jacob's scars, they weren't who he was; they were only representative of what he had been through.

"They have no future." Judith yanked especially hard on a potato, again spraying dirt over her apron. "No real future at all."

"Of course they do. It might be limited. I know that Matthew will never work in a field or build a barn, but that doesn't mean his life is useless. *Gotte* still has a purpose for his being born, for his being among us."

"Your child is what…four?"

"Nearly five."

"My Rachel is eight. Come back in three years and let's see if you're still so optimistic."

Hannah would have offered a hand of comfort to the woman, because her words seemed to come from a place of deep pain, but Judith was back on her feet moving toward the okra plants at the end of the row. "You can leave the basket by the tools when you're done."

Jacob pushed Rachel's wheelchair as they gave Hannah a tour of the playhouse.

Hannah seemed quite taken with the child. She would repeatedly squat by the chair and ask

Rachel questions about what books she liked, who her favorite princess was, whether she enjoyed school.

"I don't always go," the young girl admitted.

Her speech was distorted by the disease, but it was easy enough to make out what she was saying if you listened. Her wheelchair had a special head pad, because she sometimes jerked back and forth. Based on what Tom, the child's father, had explained to Jacob, Rachel was better off than many of the children with CP. She could speak, could feed herself, although it required a special spoon strapped to her hand, and her intelligence was on the normal scale.

Jacob thought she was a beautiful child with a very special smile.

"School prepares people to work," Rachel continued. It was obvious she was repeating what she'd been told by someone, probably her mother. "I won't ever hold a job, so I don't have to go if I don't want to."

"I'm sure you go when you can," Hannah said.

"*Ya*, but *Mamm* says that it doesn't matter much and that if I'd rather stay home…" Rachel's right hand jerked to the side, hitting the padded rail that covered every part of the playhouse. "She says that I don't have to go. I like school, though, and *Dat* says that the teacher misses me when I'm not there."

"I'm sure she does."

Rachel grinned up at both Hannah and Jacob.

"I woke up feeling *narrisch*, but after I lay around all morning *Mamm* finally said I could come out here. I always feel better when I'm in my castle."

"Let's see this funny mirror that Jacob installed."

"It's the best."

They spent the next five minutes giggling and making silly faces in the mirror which pulled and distorted their images like taffy. Finally they wheeled Rachel back to the front porch, and Judith came out and retrieved her without a word. Rachel waved as they walked away, and Jacob assured her he'd be back the following week to see if any updates needed to be made to the playhouse.

Once they were back in the buggy, he noticed that Hannah was uncharacteristically quiet.

"Something wrong?"

*"Nein."*

"Hmmm…because you were laughing with Rachel, but now you seem quite serious."

Hannah stared down at her hands. "It's only that I spoke with her *mamm*, and it left me feeling…uncertain of things."

Jacob sighed. "I should have warned you

about Judith. She has *gut* days and bad ones. I take it today was a bad one."

"She's so bitter and angry."

"Tom thinks it's depression. He finally talked her into a seeing a doctor who did prescribe some medication, but many days she doesn't take it…or so Tom says."

"Can't she see how beautiful Rachel is? What a blessing she is? She's that little girl's mother. She should be able to look past the child's disability."

"I agree with you. All we can do is pray that she'll have a change of heart, that the medicine will work. We'll support them however we can."

"It makes me angry," Hannah admitted.

"Because you have a big heart. You care about children."

"I'm sure Judith cares about Rachel. It's only that…" Tears clogged her voice.

"Don't cry…"

They were nearly to her house. He reached over and squeezed her hand, directed the gelding down the lane, and parked the buggy a discreet distance from the front porch. "What's this about? Why the tears?"

"Because…because…" She swallowed, scrubbed both palms against her cheeks and finally spoke the words that tore at her heart. "Because I was like that."

"You weren't."

"I was, Jacob. You don't know…my thoughts, my anger at *Gotte*, even at other people…people with normal families."

"You're being too hard on yourself." He put a hand on each of her shoulders and turned her toward him. "Listen to me, Hannah. You're a kind, *gut* person, and you're a *wunderbaar* mother. But you're not perfect. No one expects you to be. I'm sure you have spent plenty of nights consumed by anger…same as me."

He waited until she met his gaze. "Same as me, same as probably everyone who has endured a tragedy."

He caressed her arms, clasped her hands in his, reached forward and kissed her softly. "But you came out the other side of that anger. Your faith and your family and your friends saw you through. Judith will find her way too. It's only taking a little longer."

Hannah nodded her head as if what he said made sense, but she quickly gathered her purse and lunch box from the floor of the buggy, whispered, "*Danki* for the ride," and fled into the house.

Hannah waited until Jacob had driven away, then she pulled in a deep breath, scrubbed at her cheeks again and squared her shoulders. She honestly didn't know why meeting Judith had affected her so. The woman was bitter and angry and hurting, but Judith's life wasn't her life.

She walked into the kitchen, surprised no one was there. Pulling the envelope with the bonus check out of her bag, she set it in the middle of the table.

Where was everyone?

She peered out the window at the backyard, garden and playhouse, but no one was there either.

Where was her mother?

Where was Matthew?

Then she heard the sound that she spent nights waiting for, the sound that she often heard in her nightmares—a wet, deep, shuddering cough that meant her son was in trouble.

She ran to his room.

Matthew was in his bed, curled on his side, facing toward her with his eyes shut.

Her mother sat beside him in a chair, and on the nightstand next to her was a basin and a cloth that she was wringing out.

"Hannah, it's *gut* you're home. Matthew isn't feeling so well."

She hurried to the bed, dropped beside it and reached to feel her son's brow. He had at least a low-grade fever, maybe more, but what sent a river of fear tumbling through her heart was the cough. He began hacking again, seemed to lose his breath and finally recovered. Opening his eyes, he smiled briefly at her and reached for her hand.

"My chest hurts," he said in a gravelly voice.

His breath came in short, shallow gasps.

"I know it does, sweetie. We're going to get you some help. You'll feel better soon. Deep breaths, okay?"

Matthew nodded and closed his eyes.

He'd fallen asleep early the night before. She should have noticed. She should have paid closer attention, but her mind had been on the audit.

"We need to get him to the hospital," Hannah said.

"It's only a cough..."

"If you'll go and get the buggy, I'll pull together his things."

She'd left early with her father that morning, left before breakfast. She'd checked on Matthew, but only for a moment and even then she'd been distracted.

Her mother still hadn't moved, though she'd set the cloth down by the basin. "It started this morning, and by this afternoon he seemed a little worse so I put him to bed. The fever is only ninety-nine."

"*Mamm*, listen to me." She turned to look at her mother and saw the fear and confusion there, so she knelt down in front of her and clasped her hands. "You did nothing wrong, but we need to take him to the hospital. We need to go now."

Her mother nodded, though she still seemed confused, dazed almost.

Hannah jumped up and began digging through Matthew's dresser for a change of clothes, the favorite blanket that he kept near him when he was sick and the book they'd been reading.

Her mother moved to her side and said, "Tell me what's happening." She reached out and covered Hannah's hands with her own. "Hannah, look at me and explain to me what is happening."

Hannah took a deep breath, tried to push down the anger and fear. "Because of the injury, Matthew's lungs don't work the same. A small cold can change into pneumonia very quickly."

"Since this morning?"

"*Ya*, since this morning."

Her mother pressed her fingers to her lips and then nodded once, decisively. "Are you sure I should hitch the buggy? Wouldn't it be quicker to call for an ambulance?"

"*Ya*, you're right. That's a better idea."

"I'll go to the phone shack right now."

She heard her mother running through the house, heard the front screen door open and then slam shut.

Hannah stopped digging through the bureau

drawer and sank to the floor next to Matthew's bed. "It'll be okay, Matthew. It'll be okay, darling."

He tried to smile at her, but fell into a fit of coughing again, and then he began to shake. "I'm so c…co…cold."

"You'll feel better soon. I promise." She pulled the covers up to his chin and pushed the favorite blanket into his hands.

It seemed only a moment before her mother returned and went into Hannah's room to pull together an overnight bag. "Stay with him. I'll get you a change of clothes. Will we ride with the ambulance?"

"I will, but you'll need to bring the buggy."

Hannah was watching out the window, praying the ambulance would hurry, when her mother walked up beside her and pulled her into her embrace. "I called the bishop too. He's praying, Hannah. Soon our whole congregation will be praying for Matthew. He's going to be all right."

Hannah blinked back hot tears and tried to smile. She needed to be strong now—needed to be strong for Matthew and for her family. They hadn't experienced this type of emergency before, and it could be upsetting—the ambulance and the doctors and the hospital. *Englisch* ways could sometimes be overwhelming and disorienting, and she couldn't begin to guess what the financial cost would be. Her mind darted away from that. There would be time enough to worry over money once Matthew was well, and he would get well.

Her father arrived as the paramedics were loading Matthew into the ambulance. He left the horse untied, still hitched to the buggy and ran toward them.

"*Mamm* will explain. I have to go." Hannah kissed him on the cheek and hopped up into the back of the ambulance.

The siren began to blare as the paramedic slammed the doors shut and then they were speeding down the road.

# Chapter Thirteen

Jacob stopped by his brother's place around dinnertime. He wanted to tell his brother about the good news with the IRS audit, and it might have been in the back of his mind that a home-cooked meal would be nice for a change. Emily could work wonders in the kitchen, especially given the fact that she did so with five boys wandering in and out of the room.

But he knew the moment that he arrived that something was wrong.

"Jacob, I was about to send Samuel over."

Samuel stood at the back door, his straw hat pushed down on his head so far that it almost touched his eyes—which would have been comical except for the somber look on his face.

"What's wrong?"

"It's Matthew."

"Hannah's Matthew?"

"He's in the hospital."

"That's not possible." He plopped down onto a kitchen chair. "I was just there, only...only an hour ago."

"It happened fast according to Sally Lapp, who heard it from the bishop."

"But—"

"Sally said it's probably pneumonia." Emily placed a glass of water in front of him and sat down in the adjacent chair. "He's at the hospital. Hannah's parents are there with her. So is our bishop and hers. Sally was planning on going up as soon as she could get there. Apparently she and Hannah have become quite close."

"I need to go. I need to be with her."

"*Ya*, you do." Emily reached out and covered his hand with hers, and that simple touch almost unnerved him.

He'd taken his family for granted for too long. He could see that now.

"I'll... I'll go straightaway."

"I want to go too." Joseph had been sitting at the end of the table reading a book from school. When Jacob looked over at him, he put a home-made bookmark in the book, shut the cover and stood up. "He's my friend. I should be there."

Samuel tried to talk his younger brother into going outside with him, but Joseph would have none of it. He crossed his arms and declared, "I'm going."

Even Emily couldn't dissuade him.

Finally Jacob said, "I'll take him and send him home with someone else if I decide to stay."

"Of course you'll stay, Jacob. Hannah needs you. Bishop Amos can bring him back. He won't mind."

"*Gut* idea."

"I would go, but…"

"Stay here, with your family. Hannah will understand."

His nephew peppered him with questions all the way to the hospital.

"How did Matthew get sick so quickly? We were just playing together last week. Was it because of something we did?" Joseph took a breath, then kept on going.

"I pushed him fast in the chair, *Onkle* Jacob. Did that cause it?"

And the most pressing question, the one that Jacob couldn't answer.

"When will he come home?"

They'd traveled for a few moments in silence when Joseph said, still staring out the window, "Matthew is like David."

"What's that?"

"Like David…in the Bible." He made the motion of winding up and letting go a slingshot.

"He's a warrior just like David, only he battles what's wrong with his body."

The hospital's lights broke through the night like a beacon, spilling out into the darkness.

Being situated in the middle of Goshen, where roughly half the population was Amish, there was plenty of buggy parking. Jacob tied Bo to the rail, assured the gelding he'd be back soon. Then he and Joseph practically sprinted into the building, through the automatic doors to the visitor information desk, then down a hall, up an elevator and down another hall.

He heard the murmur of voices before they turned the corner, and he really shouldn't have been surprised, and yet he was. The room was filled with Amish. Hannah's parents, the bishop from both her district and Jacob's, both of Hannah's sisters and their husbands and their children. Sally Lapp and her husband—Sally seemed to be knitting. Leroy was discussing crops with Tobias Hochstetler, who was Claire and Alton's neighbor. So many people, waiting on word of a very special boy.

He thought Joseph would join the other boys playing checkers, but instead he slipped his hand into Jacob's and walked with him over to Hannah's parents.

"Any word?"

"No, Jacob. Sit down. We're all still waiting to

hear from the doctor." Hannah's father tossed a newspaper onto the coffee table. "Sit. You look as if you've been rushing around."

"*Ya*, I suppose I have."

It was Joseph who stepped in front of Hannah's *mamm*, eyes wide, his small hat in his hands. "Is Matthew going to be okay?"

"Yes, Joseph. I believe he is going to be fine."

"But right now he's sick."

"Yes, he is."

"So, I can't see him."

"*Nein.* Only his *mamm* can be with him now, but I think Matthew would be very happy to know that you're here."

Joseph pulled in his bottom lip, blinking rapidly. Finally he said, "Okay. I'll just wait—over there," and he walked slowly to where the other boys were. Jacob noticed that he sat beside them, watching the game of checkers, but he didn't join in. Instead his eyes kept going to the hall, the clock, Jacob and then back to the board, as if he was afraid he might miss something.

Someone had brought a basket of baked goods, and there was coffee in the vending machines. After an hour of waiting, Jacob wandered down the hall to purchase a cup. He must have stood there for five or ten minutes, staring at the options of black, cream, cream and sugar, vanilla cream and sugar. The possibilities seemed endless, but it made no difference how he had his coffee, only that the caffeine worked to push back the fatigue. He needed to be awake and alert when Hannah called for him, and he knew that she would.

"Pretty nasty stuff," Hannah's father said, coming up beside him and staring at the machine.

"*Ya*, I remember."

"They let you drink it when you were in the hospital?"

"Not really, but occasionally I'd sneak out of my room and purchase a cup. The nurses, they don't like patients drinking caffeine after dinner. They insisted it wasn't good for us. Probably they were right, but I also think they didn't want us restless when things should be quieting down."

"How long were you in the hospital?"

"The first time…four weeks. I went back for three other procedures. Those other stays were shorter—three to five days most of the time."

"Must have been difficult."

"*Ya*. Being here, under the fluorescent lights with the constant whir and beeping of *Englisch* machines, it grated on me after a while. I think the worst part was being away from everything that was a part of my life—the farm and workshop and family." He blinked away the tears and punched the button for black coffee.

"I meant the surgeries must have been hard, the pain of the injuries."

"*Ya*, that too."

"I'm sorry we weren't there for you, son."

Jacob jerked at the use of the word *son*, or perhaps it was the touch of Alton's hand on his shoulder that surprised him.

"I barely knew you then, Alton."

"And yet you were a part of our community."

"It was after we'd divided into two districts."

"Still, we are connected through our history, through being one community before. We aren't so big that we can't still care for one another." Alton cleared his throat and chose a coffee with cream and sugar. When he turned to study Jacob, a smile pulled at the corners of his mouth. "Claire and I believe that *Gotte* brought you into Hannah's life for a reason…into all our lives. You've been a *gut* friend to her and maybe something more, *ya*?"

"I have feelings for your *doschder*, if that's what you're asking, but I'm not sure…that is, I don't know if Hannah…"

"Have you asked her?"

"About how she felt? *Nein*. It took all of my courage to ask her to Saturday's picnic."

Hannah's father laughed and steered them back toward the waiting room. "Young love presents its own challenges. You and Hannah, you will find your way."

Is that what he felt for Hannah?

Love?

Something pushed against his ribs, and he thought of the cardinal in the garden he'd seen just that afternoon, of Hannah smiling as she agreed to go to the picnic with him, of the way that Judith had brought such sadness to her, of Matthew smiling as he donned his conductor's hat and asked to be pushed out to the playhouse.

*Ya*, he did love her. He loved them both, and as soon as he had a chance he planned to make sure she knew.

Hannah had only moved from Matthew's side to use the restroom. She was aware that her parents were in the waiting room, but she didn't want to go to them until she had some answers. Matthew was still sleeping fitfully, waking every few minutes to attempt to cough the congestion up from his lungs.

A woman in a white coat walked into the room carrying a computer tablet and wearing a stethoscope. "I'm Dr. Hardin. You must be Matthew's mother." She looked awfully young to be a doctor. Her hair was cut in a short red shag, and she wore large owlish glasses.

"*Ya*, I'm Matthew's *mamm*. Is he all right? Did we get here in time?"

"You did the right thing bringing him in so quickly. Often parents wait, hoping the situation will improve on its own. In this case, your quick decisiveness probably saved Matthew a potentially long stay in the hospital."

Hannah had to sit then. Actually she fell into the chair behind her. She hadn't realized how heavy the weight of her guilt was until it was lifted from her. She felt so light that she might simply fly away.

"They explained to me when Matthew was first hurt that it was something we must watch for…" Tears clogged her voice, and she found she couldn't finish the sentence.

Dr. Hardin patted her shoulder, then moved to Matthew's side. She listened to his chest, checked his pulse, placed a hand against his forehead. Hannah knew well enough that the nurse had already done these things, and she appreciated the doctor's attention all the more for it.

She also was comforted by the fact that Dr. Hardin spoke softly to Matthew the entire time she was examining him. She seemed to understand that he was more than just a patient in a bed.

He was a young boy who was scared and hurting.

He was a young boy with a family that loved him very much.

Hannah liked this doctor and trusted her immediately.

"The chest X-rays do show pneumonia, and the CBC confirms that."

"His blood count…"

"Exactly. Since it's the bacterial form, we'll start him on some IV antibiotics, give him some breathing treatments and he should be feeling better soon." She entered data on her tablet as she spoke. Finally she glanced up and looked directly at Hannah. "I won't sugarcoat it. Children with a spinal cord injury have a harder time recovering from these events. We could be looking at a rough forty-eight hours, but if he responds to the antibiotics, Matthew will be much better within a few days."

*"Danki."*

"You're welcome. Do you have any questions?"

"Only, did I do something wrong? Where did he…catch this?"

Dr. Hardin was shaking her head before Hannah finished her question. "You can't keep him in a bubble. Matthew could have picked it up anywhere—the store, the library, even at a church service. The important thing is that you recognized the symptoms immediately."

"Only I didn't. I wasn't home today, and my mother didn't know…"

"You got him here in plenty of time, and it helps that he's a healthy young guy. Apparently he's eating well and getting plenty of exercise."

"*Ya*, both of those things."

Dr. Hardin squeezed Matthew's hand and then walked back around the bed. She stopped beside Hannah and placed a hand on her shoulder. "If you have any questions, ask the nurses or ask them to call me. I'm here most of the time, and I'll be happy to come down and talk to you."

"What happens next?"

"A nurse will come in and start the antibiotics. He needs rest to fight the infection, so expect him to sleep a lot. We'll also continue breathing treatments, and when he's strong enough we'll get him up and around—that's very important with pneumonia patients. We'll do X-rays again tomorrow to be sure that he's improving."

Dr. Hardin had made it to the door when she turned and said, "By the way, Matthew's grandparents have been asking how he's doing. They're in the waiting room down the hall. You might want to give them a status update."

Hannah nodded, but she was suddenly completely exhausted. She wasn't sure she could drag herself down there. Still, her parents deserved to know.

A nurse, an older black man who had introduced himself as Trevor, changed out the bag attached to Matthew's IV. He hummed softly as he worked, and Hannah thought that maybe he was humming a hymn...one of the old ones that both Amish and *Englisch* sang.

*I am weak, but thou art strong,*
*Jesus keep me from all wrong.*

He glanced up at her and smiled.

"That's the antibiotics that you're adding to his IV?"

"Yes, it is. Our little man didn't even wake up, which is good. He's resting. If you'd like to step out of the room, I'm sure he will be fine."

"Okay. Perhaps for just a minute..."

"Go. Matthew's fan club is quite worried."

Hannah didn't know what he meant by fan club, but she did need to speak to her parents. She took one last look at her son, pushed through the door and trudged down the hall.

Jacob happened to look up at the exact moment Hannah appeared in the waiting room. She looked so tired, so vulnerable, that he jumped up and went to her.

She raised her eyes to his. "He's going to be

okay. They think…they think we made it here in time."

The words were softly spoken, but everyone heard, perhaps because everyone had stopped what they were doing at the sight of her.

As her words sank in, there was much slapping on the back, calls of "praise *Gotte*" and nodding heads—almost as if everyone knew that would be the answer. They'd believed that *Gotte* wasn't done with young Matthew yet. His life wasn't complete.

Jacob led Hannah over to her parents, who were standing now, smiling and obviously relieved.

"Hannah, I'm so sorry that I didn't realize how sick he was. I should have…should have called you earlier. Should have rung the emergency bell or…"

Hannah pulled her mother into a hug. "You did fine. You put him into bed and were caring for him. What more could I ask?"

"So he's going to be all right?" her father asked.

"The doctor said the next forty-eight hours will be critical, but she thinks that we made it here in time."

"That's *gut*. That's such a relief," her mother said.

Her father nodded. "It is *gut*, and we'll stay

with you as long as you need us. You're not alone in this."

"I know I'm not, and I appreciate the offer, but you should all go home." Hannah turned toward the group. "*Danki, danki* all of you for coming and for praying for me and for Matthew. I appreciate it more than you know. Don't feel…don't feel that you need to stay."

But no one was willing to go home just yet.

The boys were now laughing as they played checkers.

Hannah's sisters had rushed over to hear the news and now they were hugging her and asking what things they could bring up for her the next day.

Her mom shooed everyone away and insisted that she sit and eat one of the muffins. "You have to keep your strength up, dear."

Bishop Jethro fetched her a cup of coffee.

Bishop Amos tapped his Bible and proclaimed that *Gotte* was *gut*.

Sally handed her a lap blanket that she'd finished knitting. "Hospital rooms can be quite cold. Please, take it. I didn't know who it was for when I started it, only that someone would need it. As I finished, though, these last few hours, I prayed for both you and Matthew."

It seemed that everyone wanted to offer her a word of encouragement, a touch, something to let her know that she had friends and families with her as she traveled this difficult path. But it was Jacob who stayed at her side the entire time. He didn't even consider leaving. Her pain was his pain, and her exhaustion he would try to bolster with his strength. After only a few minutes, she was ready to go back to Matthew's room.

"Can I walk you?"

"Of course."

They padded quietly down the hall, shoulder to shoulder, her hand in his.

When they finally reached Matthew's room, Hannah said, "You can come in if you like."

"Are you sure?"

"*Ya.* Matthew will ask if you've been here. He thinks of you as quite the hero."

"I'm no hero," Jacob protested.

"To that four-year-old boy lying in the bed, you are."

*And what am I to you?* The question was on his lips, but he bit it back. Hannah's attention was on her son, and she was no doubt exhausted, plus the next few days would be arduous. The last thing she needed was questions from him about their relationship.

He satisfied himself with saying, "You know, you didn't have to make a trip to the hospital to get out of your date with me."

Hannah smiled, and stared down at her hands

and then looked back up at him. Rising on her tiptoes, she kissed him on the cheek. "Oh, you think I want out of it, do you?"

"Crossed my mind."

"I could just say I have to wash my hair."

"You could."

"I wouldn't."

"That's *gut* to know." He reached out and placed his palm against her cheek.

She closed her eyes for a moment and he wondered if she missed that…the physical touch of another. She'd been married before. She knew of the intimacies between a man and a woman. Her life had to be lonelier for the loss of it.

They walked into the room hand in hand, and when Jacob saw Matthew in the bed, his heart flipped like a fish that had landed on the bank of a river. The boy looked so impossibly small and vulnerable, and yet he had the heart of a warrior. Who had said that? His nephew, on the ride over.

And it was true.

Jacob pulled up a chair and sat there, holding Matthew's hand and praying silently for the young boy. Hannah used the time he was there to go into the restroom, freshen up and go to the nursing station. When she returned with a pillow and blanket, he jumped up to take them from her and place them in the chair.

"You're going to sleep here?"

"I doubt I will sleep, but *ya*."

"You want to be with him."

"In case he wakes up. Before…sometimes he would wake up in the hospital and not recognize where he was and be frightened."

"You'll let us know if you need anything? You can call my phone in the shop. I can sleep there in case—"

"I need you to convince those people out there to go home."

"Our *freinden*?"

Hannah smiled again, the weariness momentarily erased. "*Ya*, our *freinden*. Especially the children. They have school tomorrow."

"I'll tell them you said so."

He kissed the top of her head before he left. It seemed hardly adequate to show how he felt. He would find a better way. He would show her that he loved her and then he would tell her. He would make sure that both Matthew and Hannah knew.

# Chapter Fourteen

Matthew's stay in the hospital lasted longer than anyone could have guessed. His birthday came and went. The days on the calendar slipped by, one after another, until October loomed in front of them. Matthew would improve one day only to slide back for three more. Dr. Hardin assured Hannah that this was normal, that he was fighting a particularly virulent form of bacterial pneumonia and that they were doing all of the right things.

Hannah's parents brought fresh clothes for her and would sit with Matthew to give her a few moments out of the room.

The nurses brought plates of food, even though Matthew was rarely awake enough to eat. "Then it's for you," they assured her. "You need to stay strong too."

Both bishops visited Hannah often, counseled

with her and assured her that many people were praying for Matthew.

Her sisters, brothers-in-law and nieces visited every few days. They joked that someone should install a bus line to the hospital, "We'd keep it busy with folks visiting Matthew. He's a very popular guy." Sharon and Beth both had less than two months until their babies were due, and Hannah worried that the traveling back and forth wasn't healthy for them or the babies.

"I want to get out of the house," Sharon admitted. "My girls are turning seven soon, but they think they're turning thirteen. I caught one with lipstick. Now, where did she get that?"

Beth nodded in sympathy. "Naomi went through that phase too, and I suspect she'll go through it again."

She loved having her sisters and her parents and her church family there. For the first time in a long time, she realized that she wasn't alone, that others were willing and eager to lend a hand.

But it was Jacob that she longed to see each day.

He always appeared, though the time varied. If he had a job in the area, he would stop by at lunch. If he was working at home, he'd wait until the end of the day and bring her something fresh to eat from Emily for dinner.

They didn't speak of the date that had never

happened or of the kiss in the buggy, but she thought of both often—especially in the middle of the night when she woke and couldn't go back to sleep.

Each time Jacob visited, he brought something for Matthew, and those items lined the windowsill—a wooden train, a book, a piece of candy for when he was well. The string of items was a testament to how long they'd been in this holding pattern, how long Matthew had been battling his illness, how faithful Jacob was.

He always stayed for at least an hour and allowed Hannah to vent her worries, to cry occasionally, to admit when she was discouraged or afraid or depressed. He never judged her and never questioned her faith, but instead he simply held her hand and assured her that he was there.

On the days when Matthew was better, was actually awake and talkative, they laughed at Jacob's stories of playhouses that he'd built, of getting stuck inside one that was supposed to resemble a baseball dugout, of forgetting to build a door in one that he'd designed to resemble a hobbit's home.

"What's a hobbit?" Matthew asked. He had to pull in a deep breath after he spoke, but his color was better and the doctor was talking about sending him home if his improvement continued.

"You haven't read him Tolkien?" Jacob's eyes widened in mock disbelief.

"We've been a little busy."

"Then perhaps I will pick it up from the library."

But instead of doing that, he'd purchased a copy at the local bookstore. After that, he'd read to Matthew for at least thirty minutes each day. Hannah had trouble understanding why that meant so much to her, why it touched her heart, but it did.

She admitted as much to her mother one day as she was walking her to the elevator.

"Why shouldn't it?" Her mother pulled Hannah away from the elevator. "Your heart is tender, Hannah. You've been through a lot in the last few years."

"That's an understatement."

"And for a time you closed off your feelings."

Hannah crossed her arms. She knew that her mother was correct, that it was an observation, not a criticism, but it was still difficult for her to think of the months following David's death and Matthew's accident.

"It's one thing to bring a gift to someone." Her mother reached out and pulled one of Hannah's *kapp* strings forward. "It's another thing entirely to spend time beside a bed, reading, simply bringing a small amount of joy into a person's life."

"I know it is." She sounded petulant to her own ears, sounded like a child.

"Jacob cares about Matthew. The quickest way to any mother's heart is to truly love her child." With those insightful words, she kissed Hannah on the cheek and pushed the button for the elevator.

After Matthew had fallen asleep that evening, Hannah turned on the small book light Jacob had given her and scanned back through the pages of *The Hobbit*. She'd read it in school, probably the same year that Jacob had. Always they'd had their reading after lunch, when the teacher or one of the older students would read aloud a chapter—sometimes two if they pleaded long enough and hard enough.

Matthew was a bit young for such a big tale, and yet he seemed to enjoy Bilbo's adventures, as well as the groups of dwarves and elves and goblins and trolls. As Hannah looked back over what Jacob had read to him a few hours earlier, she didn't hear the tale in the voice of Bilbo Baggins, though. Instead she heard Jacob's voice—clear and steady and strong.

She could admit to herself that she wanted that. She wanted Jacob in her life, but what she couldn't admit, what she couldn't begin to fathom, was why he would be interested in taking on her and Matthew.

And there it was—in the deepest part of her heart, beneath the fatigue and fear. In the place where her dreams resided, she was certain that Jacob would one day come to his senses and realize that he didn't want the challenge of a disabled son and a mother who was emotionally scarred.

Hannah woke Friday morning with the same questions circling through her mind.

How much was the hospital bill?

How could she possibly pay it?

Was her father's farm secure now?

Had they been able to raise enough money?

Where would they live if they were forced to move?

How would she break the news to Matthew?

Even as her heart rejoiced over the fact that Matthew was well enough to be discharged, Hannah's mind couldn't help rushing ahead to what was next.

"You're exhausted is all." Sharon had stopped by with fresh breakfast muffins. Now she sat in the chair by the window, knitting a baby blanket that was optimistically blue.

"Still hoping for a boy?"

"*Ya*, but if it's a girl, I'll give the blanket to Beth."

"And if she has a girl?"

"Someone in our church will have a boy." She pointed her knitting needle at Hannah. "And stop trying to change the subject."

"Which was?"

"Your exhaustion."

"Pretty lame subject."

"Tell me what's really bothering you."

Hannah bit her bottom lip, walked to the window and stared out at the beautiful fall day. It seemed as if she'd been in this hospital for months instead of weeks. "This incident with Matthew wasn't a solitary event."

"Meaning?"

Hannah glanced at her son, curled on his side, soft snores coming from him. "Meaning it's my life. This could happen again next month or next year. Or it could be something else entirely."

"You're saying that you're not a safe bet."

"Excuse me?"

"We're talking about Jacob, right? Because I know that you wouldn't change your life, your time with Matthew…even if it meant that you could have a perfect child, a healthy husband and a life without financial problems."

"*Nein*, I wouldn't."

"So you're worried about Jacob."

"I suppose." Hannah moved over and sat on the stool next to Sharon's chair. "Maybe you've hit the heart of the matter. This is my life. I am grateful to have Matthew, and somehow I will find a way to be strong for him."

"But Jacob?"

"I can't possibly ask him to shoulder the burdens of my life."

"Isn't that Jacob's decision?"

"He might care for me…"

"*Ya*, that kiss in the buggy seems to suggest he does."

"I wish I'd never told you about that."

"And stopping by every day…bringing Matthew and you small gifts. The man is smitten."

"Caring for someone is one thing."

"Indeed it is."

"Sacrificing the life you have for them, that's another thing entirely."

Sharon dropped her knitting into her bag, reached forward and put a hand under Hannah's chin. "Look at me, *schweschder*."

When Hannah finally raised her eyes, Sharon was smiling in her I-know-a-secret, older-sister way. "Perhaps for Jacob, you and Matthew aren't a sacrifice. Perhaps you're a blessing."

Jacob puttered around his workshop all of Friday morning. By lunch he'd finished all of his projects and stored them neatly on the shelf, cleaned off his workbench, stored his tools and even swept the floor. With nothing left to do, he walked into his office, Hannah's office, sat in her chair and asked himself for the thousandth time why she would want to marry someone like him.

He looked up when he heard a long whistle. His brother's boots clomped across the workshop floor. He stopped in the doorway of the office. "Someone has been cleaning house."

"How are you, Micah?"

*"Gut."* He plopped down into the chair across from him. "Is today the day?"

"That Matthew comes home? *Ya.* Hannah thought they would release him after lunch."

Instead of answering, Micah's right eyebrow shot up.

"Don't give me that look."

"I'm just wondering—"

"I know what you're wondering. Her parents wanted to pick them up, and…well, I thought this was a time for family."

Micah's smile grew.

"Are you laughing at me, *bruder*?"

"You remind me of a lovesick pup is all. You remind me of myself a few years ago."

*"Ya?"* Jacob didn't bother denying his observation. He felt lovesick—excited, worried, a little nauseous.

"Will she come back to work?"

"She wants to. She even asked me to bring over the box of receipts for her to work on at home until she's sure Matthew's strong enough to leave with her mother." Jacob pushed the box on the floor with the toe of his work boot.

"When are you going to ask her?"

"Ask her?"

"To marry you."

"What makes you think I am?"

"So you're not?"

"I didn't say that."

"So you are."

"*Ya*, only… I want to wait for the right time."

Micah sat forward, crossed his arms on the desk and studied his brother. "You're a *gut* man, Jacob. *Mamm* and *Dat*, they would be proud of who you've become."

Jacob had to look away then, because they were the words he'd needed to hear for quite some time. When had he become so emotional? He felt like he walked through each day without enough skin, as if his every feeling was displayed on the surface. Maybe that was because he'd spent so long hiding behind his scars. He wasn't sure if knowing Hannah had changed him or if time had, and he didn't want to go back, but he hadn't learned how to deal with the deluge of emotions.

He cleared his throat and said, "I thought I'd give her a few weeks to settle in. I don't want to rush her and she has to be exhausted, plus…"

"You're thinking about this all wrong."

"I am?"

Micah tapped the desk. "She wants to be here, working with you."

"You can't know that."

"She wants you in her life, Jacob."

"If I was certain—"

"Waiting will only cause her to worry that you don't want the same thing."

Jacob stared out the window and thought of his brother's words. Hannah did seem worried, preoccupied even. She also seemed so happy to see him. Was she concerned that one day he'd simply stop coming by? Was she worried that he'd realize the awesome responsibility it would be to father Matthew? Did she think that one day he might turn tail and run?

"When did you become so wise?"

"I've been working on it."

"What if she says no?"

"She won't."

"But what if she does?"

"Better to know now. Then you can move on."

"I don't know how to do that."

"You're getting your buggy in front of your horse."

Jacob jumped up. "You're right."

"It's *wunderbaar* to hear you say that."

"I'm going over there right now, and I'm going to ask her."

"Maybe you should shave first."

"*Gut* idea."

"A haircut wouldn't hurt, either."

"I don't have time for a haircut."

"You only ask a woman to marry you once. Why not look your best?"

"Should I wash my buggy too?"

"Wouldn't hurt."

"I was kidding."

"So was I."

Jacob stopped in the doorway. "Shouldn't I take her flowers or something?"

Micah ran his fingers through his beard, tilted his head to the left and then the right. Finally he said, "*Gut* idea. In fact, Emily already thought of it."

"She did?"

"There's a basket of fresh-cut wildflowers by the door."

"For me?"

"For Hannah."

"That's what I meant."

"But you can say they're from you. Emily asked me to bring them over so you'd have something to take with you."

"How did she know I was going to see Hannah?"

Micah shrugged. "Don't bother trying to understand women, Jacob. Just be grateful that *Gotte* created them."

Hannah's mother and father arrived at the hospital before noon.

"I get to go home," Matthew declared.

"So we heard." Alton stuck both of his thumbs under his suspenders. "Didn't realize you had so much to take with you. We might need another buggy."

"Jacob made all of those things for me."

"Did he, now?"

"Were you kidding?" Matthew pulled in a big breath. He was better, but still weak from the ordeal of the past two weeks. "Do we have enough room?"

"He was kidding," Hannah's mother assured him. "I even brought a backpack to put them in." She set the bag made from blue denim on Matthew's bed.

"I can't believe you still have that thing," Hannah said. "I haven't seen it in years."

"Why would I throw it away? I knew Matthew would need it soon."

"Was it yours, *Mamm*?"

"It was." She ran her thumb over the shoulder strap. Thinking of her school days, when she was young and innocent and naive, reminded her of how much had happened since then. The surprising thing was that she didn't feel angry like she did before. She would always miss David, and she wished that Matthew hadn't been involved in the accident, but this was the life she'd been given, and she was grateful for it.

Despite what she'd shared with her sister earlier that morning, she was grateful.

"I need to go downstairs for a few minutes. Can you two help Matthew pack up?"

"Sure thing," her mother said.

But her dad stepped out into the hall with her. "I know you've been worried about the farm."

"*Ya*, I have."

"I appreciate all you've done, Hannah. You and your *schweschders*."

"You wouldn't have needed our help if it wasn't for—"

Hannah stopped talking when her father stepped directly in front of her. He placed a hand on both sides of her face like he'd done when she was a child. His touch stopped the whirlwind of thoughts rattling through her mind.

Once he was sure that she was focused on him, he smiled and said, "We're *gut*."

"You…you had enough money?"

"We had enough. You don't have to worry about the bank loan. I stopped by the bank on the way here, and I paid all the back payments.

We even had a little extra. If you don't want to keep working for Jacob, you can stay home. If that's what you want to do."

"I enjoy the work," she admitted. "There is less to do now, though. Perhaps Jacob would let me work only two days a week, the days Matthew doesn't have physical therapy."

"That's a *gut* idea."

She stood on her tiptoes and kissed him on the cheek. "I love you, *Dat*."

"And your mother and I love you."

Those words echoed in her ears as she made her way down to the business office. She hadn't wanted to bring up Matthew's hospital bill. Her parents didn't need another thing to worry about. They had enough on their plates. Still, her heart was heavy as she checked in with the receptionist and sat waiting for her name to be called. It seemed every time she solved one problem another popped up. She knew from past experience that the hospital bill would be in the thousands, maybe tens of thousands.

She'd sunk into quite a depression when they finally escorted her back to a small, neat office. The woman's name tag said Betty, and she offered Hannah coffee or water.

"*Nein*. Matthew is waiting to go home, so I should hurry."

"I understand. Have a seat and we'll go over this quickly."

Betty was matronly, probably in her sixties, and she wore her gray hair in a bun. She paused and looked at Hannah when she spoke, and her smile seemed to go all the way to her eyes.

"I'm so glad to hear that Matthew's doing well."

"*Ya, Gotte* is *gut.*"

"All the time." Betty smiled broadly and then she opened the file.

"I have a copy for you of the printout listing the charges for Matthew's care." The stack she picked up was at least an inch thick and held together with a large binder clip. She slid the papers across the desk.

Hannah paged quickly through the printout to the last page and nearly gasped at the final amount. She'd known it would be high, but she hadn't expected…

"There must be a mistake," she said.

"I assure you, I went through the billing line by line. It's all correct."

"*Nein.* That's not what I meant. The…the total is wrong."

Betty put on her reading glasses hanging from a chain and turned to the last page of her copy of the bill.

"It says we owe nothing, but I haven't... I haven't paid anything yet. So this must be wrong."

Betty pulled off her glasses and sat back. "No one told you?"

"Told me what?"

"Kosair Charities paid for Matthew's bill."

"Why would they do that?"

Betty shrugged. "It's what they do. It's part of their mission. They understand that having a child with an SCI can be a heavy financial burden, and they try to help those who need it."

"So I don't owe anything?"

"Not a penny."

Hannah brushed at the tears streaming down her face, and Betty jumped up and fetched a box of tissues.

Five minutes later, Hannah made her way back to Matthew's room, carrying the envelope in her purse that stated their bill was paid in full.

Hannah should have taken a nap like her mother suggested, but she was too tired to sleep, which made no sense.

It felt so good to be home, to see familiar things around her, to be back in the Amish world. She kept walking through the house— looking out the window, appreciating the light breeze, relishing the lack of flickering fluorescent light, drinking her *mamm*'s fresh coffee.

Matthew was asleep.

Her mother was in the kitchen, putting together a casserole for dinner.

Her father was in the barn.

Hannah walked out on the front porch, watching for…what was she watching for?

Then a buggy turned down their lane, and she realized it was Jacob and she knew that what she'd been watching for was coming toward her.

When he handed her the basket of flowers, she laughed. "Jacob Schrock, did you pick these?"

"*Nein*. Emily did."

"Well, it was very sweet of her and you."

"How's Matthew?"

"He's *gut*—asleep right now."

"Would you like to take a walk?"

The day was mild enough that she wore a light sweater, but the sun was shining, and the leaves had fallen in a riotous display of reds, greens and gold.

"I'd love that."

As they walked, their shoulders practically touching, the leaves crunching beneath their feet, Hannah felt the last of the tension inside of her unwind. She was home, and that was good. Home and family and friends were what she needed.

But what of the man walking next to her?

Was their future to be as friends, or more?

And dare she ask him now?

They stopped when they reached the pasture fence. Dolly cropped at the grass, and a red bird lighted on a nearby tree limb. Jacob saw it, glanced at Hannah and then started laughing.

"Did I miss something?"

"I think my *mamm* is telling me to get on with it."

"Your *mamm*?"

"It's a long story."

"I've always loved a *gut* story."

Hannah was aware that her heart beat faster when she was around Jacob. She didn't know what to do with her hands—her arms felt awkward whether she crossed them or let them swing by her side. She felt like a teenager who hadn't quite grown into her limbs, and she blushed at the slightest look from him. Were those things love? Or was love the simple fact that she couldn't imagine her life without Jacob in it?

He told her about his mother and how she loved red birds and how she said they were a sort of messenger from *Gotte*.

"Did she believe that?"

"I'm not sure. She could have been teasing. On the other hand…maybe she was serious. I only know that I've been seeing red birds when I needed a nudge in the right direction lately."

"And you needed to see one now?"

They were leaning against the pasture fence, their arms crossed on the wooden beam, watching the mare. Jacob glanced sideways at her, a crooked smile pulling at his mouth. "*Ya*, I did."

Jacob knew now was the time.

He'd known it in the workshop when Micah had told him to go and see Hannah, to ask her, to face his future.

He'd known it when he'd seen Hannah waiting on the porch.

And he'd known it when the red bird had alighted on the fence beside them.

Still, it took courage to ask a girl to marry you, to spend her life with you.

His heart was hammering against his chest, and every time he glanced at Hannah his palms began to sweat. He was acting like a *youngie*, like the lovesick pup that Micah had mentioned. That image brought him to his senses. He wasn't either of those things. He was a man in love, and it was past time to find out if Hannah felt the same way.

He turned to her, clasped her hands in his own and said, "I need to ask you something."

"You do?"

"I care about you, Hannah."

"And I care about you."

"I care about you and Matthew."

"He adores you." Her voice was lower, huskier, and he thought he saw tears sparkling in her eyes. He prayed they were happy tears.

He'd lived in the past for so long that he felt as if his feet were encased in cement, his tongue was tied and his brain had stopped working completely. Somehow he needed to break free from that past.

Taking a deep breath, he squeezed Hannah's hands and plunged into his future. "Will you marry me?"

"Wow."

"Wow yes or wow no?"

"I... I wasn't expecting that."

A pretty blush worked its way up her neck. Jacob had the absurd idea that he might be dreaming this entire thing, that he might wake up and find the lovely woman standing beside him, looking up at him with those beautiful brown eyes, was a figment of his imagination.

"I'm surprised is all."

"Good surprised or bad surprised?" Before she could answer, he rushed on. "I know that I'm not a perfect man, and I would understand if you said *no* because living with me, with a man like me—"

"Do you love me?"

He'd been staring at their hands but now he

jerked his head up, reached out and touched her cheek. "Yes, Hannah. I love you, and I love Matthew, and it would be an honor to be your husband and his father."

"We love you too."

"You do?"

"*Ya*. Didn't you know?"

"I'd hoped."

He pulled her to him then, relief flooding through his soul. "You love me, Hannah?"

"Yes." She laughed and pulled back, gazed up into his eyes. "You're a *gut* man, Jacob, and a *gut* friend. I wasn't sure...wasn't sure that you'd want your life to be complicated so."

"Everyone's life is complicated, even Plain folks'."

"Matthew's crisis has passed, for now, but there will be others."

"True of any family."

"It won't be easy."

"I don't expect it to be."

"But you're sure?"

"*Ya*. Are you sure, Hannah?" He took her hand and raised it to his cheek, to his scars, held it there. "These won't bother you?"

"We all have scars. Yours are simply on the outside."

He stepped closer, kissed her softly once and then again, pulled her into his arms. They stood there, with the fall breeze dropping even more leaves around them and Jacob thought that he could feel Hannah's heart beating against his.

When she finally stepped back, still smiling, he asked, "Who do you want to tell first?"

"Matthew. Let's go and tell Matthew."

\* \* \* \* \*

*If you loved this story, be sure to pick up these other tales of Amish life and love:*

*HIS NEW AMISH FAMILY*
*by Patricia Davids*
*HER FORGIVING AMISH HEART*
*by Rebecca Kertz*
*THE AMISH SUITOR*
*by Jo Ann Brown*
*THE WEDDING QUILT BRIDE*
*by Marta Perry*
*THEIR AMISH REUNION*
*by Lenora Worth*

*Available now from Love Inspired!*

*Find more great reads at*
*www.LoveInspired.com.*

Dear Reader,

Sometimes life's burdens can seem terribly heavy, and yet we have the assurance that all things work together for the good of those that love God. He has wonderful things planned for us—the very best things—and He loves us more than we can begin to imagine.

Hannah is a young mother who had envisioned a very different future for herself—she would have a houseful of children, relish the steady and faithful love of her husband, and live a plain and simple life. But even Amish lives are touched by tragedy. When she returns home, she is reminded of the comfort of family, and she also remeets Jacob. God knows Hannah's hurts, and He is planning a future for her all along.

Jacob has endured his own tragedies, and yet to some degree he has come to terms with his solitary existence. But he doesn't see himself as God sees him—as a beautiful creation. He doesn't believe anyone would want to spend their life with him. Then one day he shows up to build a playhouse and finds his future waiting for him.

I hope you enjoyed reading *A Widow's Hope*. I would love to hear from you. Feel free to email me at vannettachapman@gmail.com.

Together may we "always give thanks to God the Father for everything, in the name of our Lord Jesus Christ" (Ephesians 5:20).

Blessings,
*Vannetta*

# Get 4 FREE REWARDS!

## We'll send you 2 FREE Books plus 2 FREE Mystery Gifts.

**Love Inspired® Suspense** books feature Christian characters facing challenges to their faith... and lives.

FREE
Value Over
**$20**

# Get 4 FREE REWARDS!

### We'll send you 2 FREE Books
### plus 2 FREE Mystery Gifts.

**Harlequin® Heartwarming™ Larger-Print** books feature traditional values of home, family, community and most of all—love.

FREE
Value Over
$20

---

**YES!** Please send me 2 FREE Harlequin® Heartwarming™ Larger-Print novels and my 2 FREE mystery gifts (gifts worth about $10 retail). After receiving them, if I don't wish to receive any more books, I can return the shipping statement marked "cancel." If I don't cancel, I will receive 4 brand-new larger-print novels every month and be billed just $5.49 per book in the U.S. or $6.24 per book in Canada. That's a savings of at least 19% off the cover price. It's quite a bargain! Shipping and handling is just 50¢ per book in the U.S. and 75¢ per book in Canada*. I understand that accepting the 2 free books and gifts places me under no obligation to buy anything. I can always return a shipment and cancel at any time. The free books and gifts are mine to keep no matter what I decide.

161/361 IDN GMY3

Name (please print)

Address                                                                      Apt. #

City                              State/Province                    Zip/Postal Code

### Mail to the **Reader Service:**
**IN U.S.A.:** P.O. Box 1341, Buffalo, NY 14240-8531
**IN CANADA:** P.O. Box 603, Fort Erie, Ontario L2A 5X3

**Want to try two free books from another series?** Call 1-800-873-8635 or visit www.ReaderService.com.

# HOME *on the* RANCH

**YES!** Please send me the **Home on the Ranch Collection** in Larger Print. This collection begins with 3 FREE books and 2 FREE gifts in the first shipment. Along with my 3 free books, I'll also get the next 4 books from the Home on the Ranch Collection, in LARGER PRINT, which I may either return and owe nothing, or keep for the low price of $5.24 U.S./ $5.89 CDN each plus $2.99 for shipping and handling per shipment*. If I decide to continue, about once a month for 8 months I will get 6 or 7 more books, but will only need to pay for 4. That means 2 or 3 books in every shipment will be FREE! If I decide to keep the entire collection, I'll have paid for only 32 books because 19 books are FREE! I understand that accepting the 3 free books and gifts places me under no obligation to buy anything. I can always return a shipment and cancel at any time. My free books and gifts are mine to keep no matter what I decide.

268 HCN 3760 468 HCN 3760

| | | |
|---|---|---|
| Name | (PLEASE PRINT) | |
| Address | | Apt. # |
| City | State/Prov. | Zip/Postal Code |

Signature (if under 18, a parent or guardian must sign)

## Mail to the **Reader Service:**

**IN U.S.A.:** P.O. Box 1341, Buffalo, New York 14240-8531
**IN CANADA:** P.O. Box 603, Fort Erie, Ontario L2A 5X3

* Terms and prices subject to change without notice. Prices do not include applicable taxes. Sales tax applicable in NY. Canadian residents will be charged applicable taxes. This offer is limited to one order per household. All orders subject to approval. Credit or debit balances in a customer's account(s) may be offset by any other outstanding balance owed by or to the customer. Please allow 3 to 4 weeks for delivery. Offer available while quantities last. Offer not available to Quebec residents.

> **Your Privacy**—The Reader Service is committed to protecting your privacy. Our Privacy Policy is available online at www.ReaderService.com or upon request from the Reader Service.
>
> We make a portion of our mailing list available to reputable third parties that offer products we believe may interest you. If you prefer that we not exchange your name with third parties, or if you wish to clarify or modify your communication preferences, please visit us at www.ReaderService.com/consumerchoice or write to us at Reader Service Preference Service, P.O. Box 9062, Buffalo, NY. 14240-9062. Include your complete name and address.

HRCBPA18R